How We Fought World War II at William T. Sherman Elementary School

by Val Dumond

… a student at

William T. Sherman School 1939-1942

Steuben Junior High School 1942-1944

The rest of the world 1944-

How We Fought World War II
at William T. Sherman Elementary School
©2012 Val Dumond

How We Fought World War II
at William T. Sherman Elementary School
Limited Edition released in 2000

ISBN-10: 0-9985489-0-1

ISBN-13: 978-0-9985489-0-6

10 9 8 7 6 5 4 3

Printed in the United States of America

Published by
     Muddy Puddle Press
     P O Box 97124
     Tacoma, WA 98497

Cover: Miss Mary Nicoud's fourth/fifth grade class, 1940. The man at the right is Principal Louis Ulrich. Can you spot the author?

What's Inside?

This one's for you, Elli!

Eleanor Lamb
1930-1952

William T. Sherman Elementary School—where Lili and her classmates learned about living with world conflict. The school served as a bomb shelter, rationing distribution center, and a place to learn how to live with others.

Preface:
A Half Century from Yesterday

IT'S ALL EXACTLY WHERE SHE LEFT IT — Lili's old neighborhood surrounding William T. Sherman Elementary School. The streets, the houses, the trees, the hospital, the huge playground (that looks much smaller now), and the school sitting up there in the center of everything like a jewel in a pendant. The trees are taller now, more filled out than those scrawny sapling branches that were still propped up in 1939 to brave the wind. They should be larger now. They've had 50-some years to grow in the center of the school's front lawn.

But look, there, there behind the school, the old steam building, just where Lili left it. Still not sure, she'd guess that the school's heating system was in there. And the small 18-inch square sign still hangs atop the fence, offering a $10 reward for information about trespassers. There after all these years.

Lili drives around the school block three times before she parks. Although she has never before driven these streets, she knows exactly where everything is. The streets are narrower than she remembered. Or are there more cars? A van chauffeured by a tense-looking woman and carrying a load of children beeps impatiently. Lili pulls over to let it pass and sits staring at the school, useless during the summer vacation.

The car faces her corner. And there she comes, emerging from the alley and walking the half-block to the school corner, holding the clenched fist of her terrified little sister. Specters from long ago, those children on their way to school.

"Don't be scared, Angel," Lili tells the smallish child. "You had fun yesterday, didn't you? You'll have fun again today. And I'll be right on the next floor above you."

The girls stop at the corner and wait for the large policeman to hold up his hands. Tony, the heavy-set Italian officer who rides up on his horse each morning to shepherd his flock to school, waves them on.

"Cross now," directs the older girl. "He'll stop the cars. See, you can do this for yourself whenever you're ready."

The cars rush by now, more than back then — back when the war effort took away steel for automobiles, rubber for tires, and gasoline for fuel. Back when everyone was fighting, in one way or another, a second world war.

Lili opens the car door and steps out slowly, taking a deep breath of the familiar air. Trees, blacktop, freshly cut grass, the heat of summer — the smell of Milwaukee.

She crosses the street and walks to the corner, to the diagonal sidewalk that leads to the building steps. No cutting across the lawn. Not allowed. She approaches the huge familiar door. Each class had its own path from the playground through one of four doors to the classrooms. Lili remembers hers well.

The doors surely must be locked during the summer. But she tries one anyway. What's this? It opens. She stands ceremoniously in the doorway and takes another deep-deep breath. Varnish, chalk, sweaty kids. It's all still here where she left it.

Inside, the woman tries to walk quietly, but her leather heels strike the terrazzo floors and set off an echo. Up the freshly waxed steps to the hard, fleck-colored hallway floors that magnify the echo. Otherwise silence. No one seems to be around.

She expects a stern looking teacher to come around a corner anytime and ask where she's going and why. But no one does. Lili walks up to the first floor where she left the principal's office. It has been moved. Otherwise, nothing else is changed. The utility closets are still there, across from the rooms that fill three of the outer areas of the square building. The fourth side faces the playground and is blocked by the steam room.

Lili walks up another flight of stairs, again fewer steps than she remembered. It was always a long walk from the first/second-grade floor to the third/fourth-grade floor, and even longer to the hallowed fifth/sixth-grade floor. Today, it's an enjoyable trip up Memory Lane.

As she approaches the second floor, Lili hears the whispers and giggles of children long gone from these halls. The specters again. There they are, on the floor, huddled over a long swath of brown butcher paper. They're coloring with chalk, filling in the outlines of figures made by the teacher. The mural depicts children from countries around the world of 1939, to show how diverse our backgrounds, how rich our history.

The figures on the grocery paper are simple and the chalk colors are vibrant, ranging from the yellow pigtails of the Dutch boy and girl to the vibrant red in the French kid's peasant skirt and the beautiful blue-green in the swirling robes of the Arabian prince.

Those were the stereotyped pictures kids made then — the Dutch children wearing wooden shoes and carrying tulips, the Russians in their fur hats watching dancing bears, the Italians carrying baskets of grapes, the English school children in short pants drinking tea, the French peasants carrying loaves of bread, the Arabs in swirling silk robes pulling at their camels, the dark skinned Africans chasing elephants, the Chinese wearing coolie hats to shade their slanted eyes, Eskimos crawling out of igloos to greet polar bears, American Indians in feathered bonnets and deer-skin clothing standing in front of teepees — an international depiction of a child's world — before The War.

Where are they all now? Those children of pre-war immigrants, those children and grandchildren escaping with and without their families from the horrors of Europe?

Lili almost expects to see them come trooping down the side streets half-walking, half-running toward the majestic schoolhouse. "They'd be much older now, of course," Lili says to herself. Her thoughts meander. I've been to three class reunions and I'm still surprised at how much the others changed while I... aren't any of them coming to this reunion? Are they still alive?

She remembers watching the rickety old folks returning for their 50th high school reunions, back when she was in high school. The few who returned looked on the brink of....

I wonder how many of our class of 1948... let's see, there were a few hundred in our graduating class... how many are alive? How many will make it back to our reunion? I'm surprised there aren't more wandering around here... around the grounds of William T. Sherman Elementary School.

"That year we entered fourth grade — on the second floor — let's see, that was just past Labor Day 1939...."

Hello Milwaukee

BERLIN, GERMANY September 1, 1939 — Hitler's mighty armies rumbled into Poland today in Panzer tanks and on foot to rescue that country from the clutches of non-Aryan alliances formed by the British with the infamous Munich Treaty. Chancellor Hitler reports that the people of Poland now are free.

HELLOOO! HELLOOO! Lili and her little sister ran from empty room to empty room in the new house, calling out the word and listening to the echo. In the cavernous living room the girls found a fireplace. "Ooh look, Mama, a fireplace with logs in it."

"Those aren't real logs, Angel," Lili told her sister.

"Yes they are."

"No they aren't, are they Mama?" Lili asked her parents as they walked through the door.

"Well, yes and no," Lili's father answered. "They look like logs, but they're not made of wood and they don't burn. See here? A gas vent. This is a gas fireplace that only looks like it burns wood."

"See?" Angel stuck out her tongue at Lili.

Younger sisters are such a bother to a nine-year-old. "See that? I was right. They're not real logs."

"Are too, Daddy says so."

"Are not." Lili ran to find the bedroom she would share with her sister. "HELLOOO!" she shouted through the hallway. "Hellooo!" came the echo, only smaller because the bedroom was small.

"I get the bed near the window." Lili staked out her claim. Lili and Angel had shared bedrooms as long as Lili could remember. With each move as she got older, Lili had hoped for a room of her own. What must it be like to be an only child? At least here, next to the window, she could watch the moon and stars as she fell asleep.

Next to the window, Lili could pull in the fading light just long enough to write in her diary. Notes to herself that would keep for sometime in the future when she became a real journalist. For now she was Lili Deveroux, Girl Reporter, making notes about her life. But one day she longed to become Brenda Starr, glamorous adventuring Reporter!

The neighborhood in northwest Milwaukee in 1939 was practically at the city's outskirts. The Deveroux family moved into the house in the 2800 block on 50th Street, between Hadley and Locust, a pleasant tree-lined street that seemed wider then because few cars were parked on it. (The few cars that belonged to residents were garaged in the back alley.) Down the street sat St. Joseph's Hospital, which drew much of the traffic. The neat looking houses were single family or duplexes set back from the street and landscaped with shrubbery and fir trees.

Milwaukee was the first large city Lili had lived in. Rosemary Deveroux had sat her daughters down and warned them of the changes they could expect, different from the small towns they had lived in, things like "noise and buses and sirens and people, lots of people. Folks live in houses with other folks," Mother had explained.

"We'll live in an apartment on the ground floor with another family living on the second floor. You girls will have to be quiet so we won't bother them."

Lili's little sister Angel had looked at her big sister for reassurance. Lili had tried to look brave, confident. Now, sitting on the floor in the empty bedroom, Lili calmed her sister's fears. "Don't worry, Ang, we'll be all right. Just look at the size of this room, much bigger than the last. As long as you remember to stay on your side!"

On that moving day, after establishing her space in the bedroom, Lili wandered about the yard with her father as they awaited the moving truck. A lacy linden tree shaded the backside of the house and faced a luxurious purple clematis that followed a fanned trellis up the side of the garage. Morning glories climbed the adjacent garage wall, a backdrop for the bright poppies, marigolds, and zinnias. The morning glories had popped out in full array of purple and white to enjoy the coolness of the early day.

"Any kids?" Angel asked leaning out the bedroom window.

"Haven't seen any," Lili answered. "But I see a tricycle next door." She pointed to the yard beyond a fence lined with fringed asters, bright snapdragons and pink and white flax. "Come on out and take a look at these flowers," she beckoned as she squatted, Indian style, to be nearer the flowers. "The bell-like blossoms taste sweet when you suck them. And Daddy says that's a peach tree."

In the corner of the yard back near the garage was a small tree about Lili's height that leaned toward the alley fence. "Look, there's a real peach on it. And another, and another. I didn't know they grew this far north; I thought they only grew in Georgia," Lili said as she reached over and plucked a juicy ripe peach from the bough.

For years afterward when Lili ate a peach she tasted Milwaukee. Whether she was remembering the peach she ate that day directly from the tree or the one Mr. Perlman sold at his friendly grocery store on Center Street, she was never sure. The peach she ate that day was small. Still, the first bite of a juicy peach would ever after evoke for Lili the sweet taste of Milwaukee on that first September day in 1939.

"Wisconsin isn't exactly one of the warmer states," her dad said. "But sure, peaches grow here." Lili wanted to be a farmer just like her dad and know everything about plants and trees and corn and cows. She had asked him why a peach tree was growing in their yard.

"They're not so different from those other trees that you see leaning out over the alley… definitely apple or plum trees," he said looking down the alley. "I betcha they tempt more than one of the neighborhood kids every fall."

"I don't remember having a fruit tree in our yard before."

"Oh yes, remember the apple trees we had in Shiocton? Those were some good pie apples."

"Sorry, Pop, I don't remember much about Shiocton. I was too young."

Moving was standard operating procedure by the time Lili was nine. This was her fifth move since she was born; her father, George Deveroux, had been born and raised on a farm, before he became a teacher. He had just accepted a job as an Agricultural County Agent in

Milwaukee County, a position that confused Lili. "Why couldn't he stay a teacher?" she asked her mom.

"He's moving up to earn a better salary," was the answer.

"Lili," called Angel from the door, her sweater in hand. "Let's go exploring."

"Is it all right, Dad?"

"Sure, let me know what you find. And don't get lost." Just then the moving truck rumbled to a stop in front of the house and a mover swung open the huge doors. "Go ahead," urged Lili's father. "The movers are here."

The girls were wandering about the backyard when the children next door appeared in their yard with their mother. They came over to the fence, the small one holding tightly to her mother's hand. The plump woman, her blond hair woven into thick braids around her head, spoke to her children with a thick German accent. To Lili and Angel she said, "Come over and meet my children."

Lili took her sister's hand as they shyly walked around to the alley gate. The jolly neighbor woman took the girls into an immaculate and delicious-smelling kitchen and introduced her children, Wilhelm, a strapping boy of twelve, and his sister, Francine, a beautiful curly-headed blond girl of three. "I am Mrs. Ludwig," she added, using a long-u and pronouncing the *w* like a *v* — Lood-vig.

While Francine clung to her apron, Mrs. Ludwig handed warm cookies to each of the children. Then Wilhelm invited his new neighbors outside. There he showed them rows of roses and tomatos. "Those are my dad's," he said proudly.

"My dad says they're hard to grow," Lili offered. "These look beautiful. Your dad must have a green thumb."

"Yeah," Wilhelm answered. "Both roses and tomatos like sunshine and they take a lotta care and roses can turn black overnight if they're not cared for. The tomatos keep black spot from happening."

"You seem to know a lot about plants," Lili said.

"My dad shows me stuff." Quickly he turned as if to change the subject, reached out toward Angel, and tapped her shoulder. "You're It!" he called over his shoulder as he ran away.

Lili and Angel felt welcome enough to join Will and Francine in a game of tag, then sat in a kind of playhouse to dress up a family of dolls. It was late morning before the girls returned home to find boxes and furniture piled in the center of all the rooms.

LITTLE BY LITTLE THE BOXES began to disappear and furniture seemed to find their own places. The piano was moved into what Mother called the Solarium — a window-lined room facing east, just the place for her houseplants. Dad's roomy easy chair with matching footstool and Mother's wicker rocker were in the living room facing the fireplace with its gas apparatus. The large family radio stood on the floor next to the chairs so everyone could listen. Dad's books found places on shelves next to the fireplace and Mom's what-nots began to line up on the mantle.

Work or not, at noon Lili's mother called a halt for lunch. Their dad had found Mr. Perlman's grocery on Center Street and brought home fresh bread, peanut butter, milk, bananas, and… more peaches. The girls perched on boxes to enjoy their food.

Food was packaged differently in those days. Peanut butter was sold in bulk from a large barrel and somehow tasted better than it ever did since then. The bread was white Wonder Bread, and the milk was delivered in glass bottles. Everyone ate their fill.

Mother cleared away the napkins and piled the dishes in the sink — she had unpacked just enough dishes so they didn't have to eat on paper plates. Lili's dad asked if the girls wanted to explore the basement with him.

"Sure," said Lili, eagerly heading toward the back door.

"Uh, no, I don't think so," Angel held back.

Her mother intervened, "I think Angel needs to lie down for a bit. She's had a busy morning." The seven-year-old threw a grateful smile at her mother and went into the bedroom.

Lili and George Deveroux walked down the dark back steps, cautiously feeling along the wall for a light switch. At the bottom, her dad found the switch and Lili discovered a rather spacious, dimly lit laundry room. There her Mom would run her weekly Monday morning race to the clothesline. "I nearly was first to get my sheets on the line this morning," Mom would announce proudly at lunch on some Mondays. One day she would grin widely and proclaim, "I got my sheets on the line before any of the neighbors this morning."

Lili found a coal bin with great heaps of black briquettes awaiting the furnace in winter. Periodically during the cold months a bulky truck would pull up in the alley behind the house. Out would hop two soot-covered men who grabbed a pair of coal hods and wheeled load after load of coal from the truck to the basement window. There they dumped the coal through the window, down the slide, into the bin. When it was full, one man hung their hods on the side of the truck as the other knocked on the door to collect his money, then they drove off. The furnace in the center of the basement would soon devour all that coal and the sooty men would return with another load. On that hot summer day, however, the coal bin sat black and silent.

In another corner of the dark basement, Lili found a larder — shelves to hold the jars of vegetables and fruit that her mother canned each fall. Soon it would hold Mason jars full of corn, peas, beans, tomatos, beets, and maybe sauerkraut. Definitely strawberries, raspberries, plums, pears, and peaches. Her mother loved to can and took great pride in providing fresh-from-the-garden treats in mid-winter.

Coming up out of the darkness and back at ground level, Lili noticed a strange little compartment next to the outside door. "For milk bottles," her dad explained. "So they won't freeze outside in winter." She opened a tiny door and found a small space and a tiny door that opened from the outside. Such useful ideas to be found in the city!

She followed her dad up the stairs, then up a second flight, and still another, to discover the attic. Here was space to store unused household furnishings, rugs and winter clothing in summer, and summer clothing in winter. It also turned out to be a great place to play on rainy days. That day her dad was carrying boxes to store for the winter.

The long day finally ended and Lili's mother called for her to come set the table. Lili could barely recall how the apartment had seemed that morning when she and Angel had run through the empty rooms yodeling and listening to the echos. Now furniture sat amid boxes that spewed their contents in all directions. In the large kitchen, Mother flew about among the boxes as she prepared dinner. She had worked hard all day lining shelves and putting utensils in drawers, and now was ready to provide a hot supper for her family; she considered it part of her job.

Lili watched her mother prepare a peach cobbler for dessert before she set the table. She wondered if she would ever learn how to cook for other people — her own family perhaps. It all seemed so complicated. Maybe if she became a writer, as she planned, she wouldn't have to cook. She could hire someone to cook for her, like she had read about in one of her Nancy Drew mysteries.

When the family finally sat down at the supper table in the kitchen, they enjoyed a full meal of pork chops, potatoes and gravy, fresh peas, and carrots, including Mom's special peach cobbler and each others company. Exhausted from the day's work, the grownups talked little, leaving the conversation to Lili and Angel, who recounted all they had learned about the neighborhood.

"I heard a European accent in Mrs. Ludwig's speech," Lili announced.

Her mom commented casually. "Is she from Germany?"

"I don't know," Lili replied. "She bakes German strudel and German cookies. She says *ain't*; I guess she must be German."

"I heard her say something bad about the Germans," Angel offered.

"What do you mean?" Daddy asked.

"I heard her say the Germans were bad people."

"Oh dear, you must be mistaken."

"They march roly-poly."

"Roly-poly?" Mom asked.

"I think so," Angel answered. "She said the darned Germans…"

"Angel, watch your tongue," Mom admonished.

"Sorry. But she said it, not me. She said the d… Germans marched roly-poly and they had no right to be there."

Dad let out a laugh. "She means the Germans marched into Poland. I heard it on the radio tonight. That must be what Mrs. Ludwig meant. Funny she wouldn't be proud of her own people."

Lili put down her fork. "Why did the Germans march into Poland?" she asked.

"The newscaster said it was retaliation for the British signing a treaty," her dad answered. When no one commented, he continued, "They'll be sorry for that one, I'll bet. The British. They'll regret that treaty with Munich."

No one seemed to understand what Dad was talking about. He liked to listen to the news on the radio by himself as he read the evening paper. If something important happened, they knew he'd tell them about it.

"I wonder if the people upstairs are German too. Their name is Rosenberg. It seems we've moved into a rather German neighborhood," Mom said.

"Nobody's been home all day upstairs," Lili said. "Where are they? Who are they?"

"Ah, we have a mystery to solve." Mom loved mysteries and had read most of Agatha Christie and Erle Stanley Gardner. She also enjoyed a radio program called "I Love a Mystery", which she listened to while she prepared dinner. "We'll have to call in Jack, Doc, and Reggie to solve this one," she suggested as she rose to clear the table.

"Oh, Mama, that's just a story," Angel smiled as she pretended to scold her mother.

"You're just repeating what Mama always says," Lili teased her sister.

"Am not. The radio tells lots of stories."

"What's most important now is getting ready for school on Tuesday," Mama cut off the debate.

"Don't we have a few more days?" Lili whined.

"Just a couple. Labor Day is Monday and school is Tuesday," she said. "Darling, can you find the box marked SCHOOL?" she called over her shoulder as she placed the dishes in the sink. She always — almost always — called her husband "Darling".

"What's in it?" he asked, "as if I didn't know."

"The new dresses I made for the girls this summer. I hope they haven't grown much since July. And the shoes. Their new school shoes are in that box. I bought them just before we left. They can't have outgrown them in just a couple weeks."

OTHER EVENTS WERE TAKING PLACE that last weekend of summer 1939 in other parts of the world. On the Friday morning that the Deveroux family were moving into their new house in Milwaukee, the tyrant Hitler was moving his troops into Poland. By Sunday, September 3, Britain and France had declared war on Germany. In the United States, few took notice of European problems. Monday was Labor Day, a festive holiday that ended summer and signaled the beginning of the school year.

Across Milwaukee, people were enjoying picnics and outings with their families. Oh, the succulent sausages and bratwurst and fried chicken and potato salad and ice cream that were digested throughout that day in parks and backyards across the city.

However, Lili didn't put these things into her diary that Labor Day. Instead, she wrote about her mounting discoveries of the day. Foremost was her discovery of the upstairs neighbors.

Labor Day was the day the Deveroux family met the upstairs neighbors — Robert Rosenberg and his mother Gertrude. A taxi dropped them at the front door late on Monday. Lili had never known anyone who traveled in a taxi. They stopped briefly at the Deveroux's door to greet their new neighbors, then hurried upstairs. After that, they emerged only briefly on Fridays to walk to the grocery store and on Sunday afternoons to walk around the block. The Deveroux family didn't know what the Rosenbergs did in between. Robert, they would learn later, was an accountant. His mother had been a nurse in her native Germany. The two of them had moved to Milwaukee at the close of World War I following the death of their husband/father in the war. They didn't talk much about that life.

On Tuesday, September 5, 1939, Lili and Angel
slipped into their new dresses, tied up their new shoes,
grabbed each others hands and, guided by their mother,
headed off to their first day at William T. Sherman
Elementary School.

Hello, William T. Sherman Elementary School

LONDON, ENGLAND, September 5, 1939 – Great Britain is rallying its troops behind the government's declaration of war on Germany. Hoping to forestall Hitler's march across Austria, Czechoslovakia, Albania, and now Poland, Prime Minister Neville Chamberlain has ordered leaflets to be dropped in the occupied countries, informing citizens of England's backing. Some government officials are calling for the resignation of Chamberlain in light of his support for the now defunct Munich Treaty.

CLOSE YOUR EYES, YOU WHO ENTERED FOURTH GRADE in September 1939. Can you see your teacher in a brand new smock? smell the fresh varnish oozing out of desks and through the halls? feel the dryness of the chalk on your fingers? taste the fresh peanut butter in your lunch? sense the tenseness of new faces? run your fingers over the pages of a fresh new never-before-touched book?

For Lili, that first day held two concerns. First of all, she was a new kid in school… again. Secondly, a war was brewing in another part of the world. She was anxious only about the first.

Lili was up early so she'd have time to fiddle with her hair. Since her ninth birthday that summer, Lili had convinced her mother to let her straight dark-brown hair grow out. Always before her mother had bobbed it just below her ears. Now it almost covered her neck. She held back the front part with a turtle shell barrette. All too often, the barrette came loose and let the unruly front hair fall across her eyes. But Lili didn't care, as long as the hair was growing out. Soon she could fix it like she knew older girls did. Maybe then it would curl.

The Deveroux daughters left the house with their mother that Tuesday morning, the three holding hands and swinging them in unison. The girls wore the new cotton print dresses their mother had sewn for them, identical, except for the colors; Lili's was a blue and purple flower print that made her brown eyes and hair seem even darker, and Angel's was yellow and brown, playing up her blue eyes and light brown hair. Lili walked with shoulders held straight, bravely hiding the swirling cyclone that was going on inside her. Angel hesitated, sometimes even stopping in mid-step to grab a stronger hold on her mother's hand. Rosemary led them along the path that Lili and Angel would take every school day for the next three years: to the alley, down to Locust Street, then over to 51st — where Lili got her first glimpse of William T. Sherman Elementary School.

The building was large, square, made of red brick and set on a slight rise of land in the center of a city block. Two angled walkways, one from each corner, reached up toward two banks of steps that rose to two doors. Lili could see the large asphalt playground behind the building, protected from the street by a low pipe fence that surrounded it. Newly planted sapling maple trees decorated the sloping front lawn.

Other children appeared suddenly, seeming to come toward the school from all directions. Why hadn't Lili seen any of them before?

At the corner she looked up at a huge police officer, the largest man (and possibly the first uniformed police officer) she had ever seen. He stood in the center of the intersection directing traffic, what little there was. He held up his arms, his hands telling cars to stop while the children crossed the street. "Hi, Tony," some boys shouted. "Hi," the smiling policeman called back, adding a friendly, "Move along, cross now." Fascinated, Lili wanted to stay and watch, but Mother tugged her toward the school.

In the next couple of years she'd get to know Tony and his slow lumbering ways. She'd watch his horse carry him slowly toward the intersection each morning. She'd notice the way the big man dismounted from the huge roan, the way he slipped the bag of oats over the horse's head before walking his plodding steps toward the center of the street. Both Tony and his horse moved slowly, a kind of sauntering. When all the children were safely in the schoolhouse, Tony would stroll back to his horse, remove the oats bag, give a mighty leap up, then ride off, leisurely clip-clopping down the street. Lili often wondered if Tony ever wanted to trim off some of his big stomach and get back to chasing crooks. Probably not.

That first morning Lili took charge after her mother waved goodbye just outside the office door. She quickly learned the layout of the classrooms: first and second graders on the first floor; third and fourth graders on the second; and the big kids — fifth and sixth graders on the third, top floor. She pulled Angel into her second grade classroom on the first floor, then climbed the marble steps to her own fourth grade room.

While she felt sure of herself when shepherding Angel, Lili felt only fear as she entered her new classroom. She shouldn't have worried.

There she was greeted by Miss Lillian Horne, a grandmotherly gentle skinny woman who liked to wear ribbons in her hair and colorful smocks. She'd soon learn that Miss Horne was very kind, extremely patient, and always cheery, like fourth grade teachers are supposed to be.

"Take that seat over by the window," her new teacher directed. A tiny woman with a sharply lined face and bony hands, Miss Horne wore bright red-striped ribbons in her hair that first day of school. Her smock was a pale print of bluebirds sitting on leafy green tree limbs. Lili felt relieved that she had a teacher she was sure she was going to like. At least she was relieved for a few minutes.

Lili wanted to shrink into thin air as Miss Horne took her arm, pulled her gently through the room, past four rows of desks filled with chattering children, to the third desk from the front in the window row. Everyone else seemed to know everyone else. They greeted each other as old friends after a very long summer.

The bell rang and Miss Horne quieted her students. "Welcome to the fourth grade," she announced as she closed the door and walked to her desk. "We have a new girl in our class this year." She smiled at Lili who tried to scrunch down behind her desk. "Her name is Lili Deveroux. Stand up, Lili, and tell us where you are from?"

The new girl knew the routine. Stand up and tell these strange faces where you came from. She had done it every other year she was in school, twice last year, always the new girl. Why didn't she ever learn to do it without a queasy stomach?

She straightened her knees and ran her hand across her face before quietly murmuring, "River Falls." She sat down abruptly.

Children know there is one thing worse than having a teacher you can't stand. That's having a teacher who knows your family. To Lili's surprise, Miss Horne turned out to be an old friend of Lili's family. Why hadn't her mother warned her?

Miss Horne continued the introduction. "Lili and her family just moved here from upstate. I knew Lili's grandmother; we both grew up in a small town up north. When I visited her last summer, I learned that this bright little girl, with a name like mine, would be in my class. You can imagine how happy I am to have my friend's granddaughter in my classroom."

Lili began to think Miss Horne would never stop. She wanted to disappear.

"That makes Old Lady Horne *Grandma's Pet*, doesn't it," a voice whispered in Lily's ear. She turned just enough to find a wide grin on the face of the boy sitting behind her. She giggled in her embarrassment, but not enough to attract Miss Horne's attention. Mercifully, the teacher had finished with Lili and was going on about life in northern Wisconsin.

The introduction concluded, Miss Horne took the roll. Lili learned that the boy sitting behind her was named Harold… Harold Hoffman. At recess she got a better look at him and found a set of friendly soft brown eyes and black hair, like hers, and stars. They walked out to the playground together, in line, one behind the other, but Lili never spoke to him. A shy girl without brothers, she found it difficult to talk to boys.

The voice came from behind Lili. "Hi-ho! My name's Megan, what's yours?"

"Lili." She turned to look into the bright sapphire blue eyes of a pale blond-haired girl, wearing the prettiest smile she had ever seen.

"You're new here. You're very lucky to have Miss Horne. I think she's a super teacher."

"Sure." The girls walked slowly out of school for recess.

"You don't talk much, do you?"

Lili nodded.

"Well, I'm the caretaker type. I look out for the lost and alone. Mother calls me the I'll-show-you-where-everything-is girl." Sure enough, Megan grabbed her hand and led Lili around the playground, pointing out the jungle gym, the painted hopscotch forms and the basketball hoops. Next she dragged Lili over to the backside of the school and showed her the giant chimney over the heating plant. The area was fenced in and carried a sign that offered a $10 reward for information leading to the arrest of trespassers. Though the girls didn't understand "trespassers", they did know the meaning of "arrest" and duly kept their distance.

"It's shady over here, not so hot," Megan said as she pulled Lili to the west side of the school out of the glare of the warm September sun. "We can sit on the railing and I'll ask you a bunch of questions, like how you like Milwaukee and what your dad does. Mine works for Harley-Davidson; he rides motorcycles and tests them. He looks like General Eisenhower. We come from New England and we're Irish, Protestant-not-Catholic."

Lili followed Megan to the railing and climbed up. She'd do a lot of that in the years to come — follow Megan. Lili soon found her voice and the two became best friends before recess ended. While both girls were blessed with curiosity, it was Megan who had the gumption to act on hers.

Megan was the kind of girl who stood out in a room crowded with children, partly because of her sparkling bright blue eyes and her wispy blond hair, a sharp contrast to Lili's thick dark brown hair. Megan wore her hair long so it could blow in the wind at times and frame her pale face at other times. What stood out the most was the way she smiled and looked right at you — like a song. Megan sang, she didn't speak.

Where Lili was serious, Megan laughed a lot. Megan talked to everyone, people on buses, shopkeepers who she knew by name, even boys. Lili seldom spoke unless someone asked her something. Megan's way of talking to anybody and everybody impressed Lili. Both girls liked to do things, but Lili pulled back while Megan dared. Lili's friend was almost her opposite. Together, they couldn't resist experimenting with life.

The two friends would meander all over Milwaukee in the months that followed, walking into strange stores and offices, pressing their noses to the windows of interesting shops. They walked together into a Jewish fish market one day. With Megan leading, the girls strolled past the rows of fish imbedded in ice, their glassy eyes staring into space. The girls tried to appear like customers, and after they had checked out all the glassed cases and open bins, Megan shook her head and took Lili's arm, "No, I don't think I want fish today," she declared loudly. Outside the girls clutched at each other and howled with laughter.

"You're too bold," Lili squeaked out between gulps of laughter.

The girls explored a synagogue, a Catholic church, a stockbroker's office, a Chinese restaurant, and a radio station, all new and exciting places that Lili had never seen before. Lili assumed at first that Megan had already been to all those places before. What she would soon learn was that Megan was exploring too.

A few days after meeting Megan, Lili met her parents. Megan's father did look like General Eisenhower, the famous Army general, as Megan had suggested. The resemblance was heightened by the khaki Eisenhower jacket Mr. Murphy wore as part of his work with the military. He taught soldiers how to operate motorcycles in or near battle zones, and in the ensuing years would often be mistaken for the famous general.

Megan's mother was a gentle, plumpish woman who wore her gray hair in a stationary set of waves and curls. Both of Megan's parents spoke with thick New England accents. "I'm a love child," Megan was fond of explaining. "My parents had me when they had almost given up ever having children." Lili had thought her own mother was older than other mothers, but Megan's mom seemed even older. The two women soon became as good friends as their daughters.

Because Megan was an only child, Lili expected her to be spoiled. Hadn't her mother criticized single children as being spoiled? True, Megan was cherished and pampered, but she was anything but spoiled. "I have a health problem," Megan confided to Lili. "I'm anemic."

"What's that?" Lili had asked.

"You know, my blood is thin. It's because I'm a late-born love child," she insisted. "Mama says I'm delicate and special." Lili never disagreed. She knew at once that Megan was special.

Lili's friend liked to pick up stray animals as often as she picked up stray people. Mrs. Murphy told Lili how often Megan brought people home because she liked them and wanted them to meet her parents. Her daughter was especially fond of old people and children, stopping to play with them, share herself for a moment.

Megan was probably as daring as Lili was reticent. Over the next few years they shared adventures, secrets, surprises, homes and lives. Wherever Megan led, Lili followed.

They went to the movies almost every weekend, sometimes both Saturday and Sunday afternoons. Lili would walk to Megan's house just off Center Street on 47th, pick her up and head for the Uptown Theater on North Avenue. Both girls loved movies and made going to them a production. They pretended to be princesses entering their private castle.

The Uptown Theater, an elegant palace of a theater, was enjoying its years of grandeur. Decorated in gold and red velvet, the magnificent richly carpeted lobby featured a romantic wide staircase that led to the mezzanine. The girls delighted in playing the grandes dames who swept up and down the stairs during intermissions to visit the Ladies' Lounge, another splendid room of mirrors and plush carpeting. On the way, they were always aware they might run into some boys from school. If they did, they tried to appear nonchalant and uninterested before they turned and trailed the boys to find out where they were sitting.

In the darkened theater, Lili and Megan poked each others ribs at the love scenes, cheered the heros, belly-laughed at Abbott and Costello and cried buckets of tears at the war stories. Megan always seemed to know the story behind the story. She explained the courage of the nurses at Bataan and she seemed to know about the Sullivan family — the five sailor brothers who were lost at sea. She told Lili about the underground networks of freedom fighters in almost every European country. And Lili always felt Megan was on personal terms with the rabbi, minister, and priest who gave up their life jackets and sank to a watery grave together aboard a torpedoed Navy ship. Megan seemed to have a mystical connection to the world's heros.

After the show, the girls always snacked on ice cream sundaes at the shop next door before heading home, reviewing the movies along the way.

On one spring Sunday afternoon that begged for adventuring, Megan felt too full of energy to sit in a stuffy theater. The girls walked right past the theater and headed up North Avenue, a street they normally didn't travel. They looked in windows of the locked stores, discussed imaginary purchases, gazed at bakery bread, sniffed at the stalls in front of the Jewish fish market, and dawdled at a used-book store before Megan spotted their destination.

A bowling alley in the early 1940s was a mysterious place, not a likely habitat for young girls. The one they spotted was small, its front windows shaded with blinds. Megan and Lili peered in the partially open door and saw... nothing. The interior was too dark, their eyes still blinded by the bright sunshine. "We'll have to go in to see," Megan whispered.

"Do you think we should?" Lili asked.

She might have saved her breath. Megan already was pulling her through the doorway, chiding her friend, "If you're half the girl reporter you claim, you'll come along and keep your eyes open. Here's a chance for a real scoop, the real inside story."

The girls tip-toed a few steps, then stopped to let their eyes adjust to the dimly lit room. Their flair for the dramatic and their familiarity with movies led them to wonder if they had stumbled into some kind of evil den. Only a rumbling sound followed by the tink-chunk chunk-tink clearly told them that this must be a bowling alley. Slowly a shape took form, a counter that blocked the view of the place where the sounds originated. They crept closer, around the counter, and there they saw, right in front of their eyes — bowling alleys with pins sitting at the end. A few afternoon bowlers were using two lanes and the girls watched wide-eyed as one man sent a ball rolling across the polished floor to crack into the pins, spilling them in all directions. They could dimly make out a boy scrambling to pick up the pins and ball, reset the pins, and send the ball back to the bowler.

"I expected more smoke and noise," Megan whispered.

"I didn't know what to expect," Lili whispered back.

"Now what do we do? Do you want to bowl?"

"I don't know how. Anyway, we don't have enough money. This would cost a fortune. Let's go before somebody sees us." The scaredy cat was becoming anxious.

With good reason. As they turned, a dark-haired man walked toward them with, of all things, a cigar sticking out of his mouth.

"Help you ladies?" he asked, not sounding either angry or scary. Still, Lili wanted to get out of there fast.

She began, "No, thank...," before Megan found her voice and piped up, "Yes, we're interested in learning to bowl. Do you know how?"

"Uh, yes, I do," he answered, surprised at the boldness of this very little girl. "In fact, we're about to have a lesson. Would you two like to sit in?"

"Yes, oh yes. That would be grand." Megan clapped her hands and turned to Lili, "wouldn't we?"

So they did, spending the rest of that Sunday afternoon listening to a lecture on the art of bowling. Although it didn't help either one very much since they had never touched a bowling ball. Yet they felt very grownup sitting with others, listening to the helpful tips.

Megan did that a lot — dragged Lili into situations she never would get into by herself, situations Lili allowed herself to be dragged into and often ended up enjoying.

Like the time one summer when Megan pulled Lili right up to Dennis Morgan, the handsome tenor movie star, after he finished an Under the Stars concert in Washington Park. Megan actually spoke to that dashing screen idol as he emerged from the stage entrance, looking handsome wearing a stylish gray topcoat casually draped over his broad shoulders, a fedora jauntily perched atop his head. The star didn't answer, but never mind; Megan had spoken to him and even touched his sleeve.

The girls spent many hours in Washington Park, rowing boats in summer, ice skating in winter and meandering through the zoo all year around. Music always emanated from the boat house — sprightly summer music for rowing and Viennese waltzes for ice skating. Hearing the music piped into the frosty air, Megan and Lili would grab mittened hands and skate in tandem to "Tales of the Vienna Woods", "Blue Danube", even "Walking in a Winter Wonderland".

"Someday I'm going to be an Olympic figure skater, just like Sonja Henie," Lili confided to her friend. To emphasize her statement, she skated out ahead and bent over in a swan figure, one leg extended straight out behind, her arms spread and slightly fluttering.

"Me too," shouted Megan, and went into her own version of the swan.

On sweltering summer days, Megan and Lili rented boats and rowed across the same lagoon where they skated in winter. There were always the inevitable bumping contests when they ran into (literally) friends sharing the same pond. The zoo was a great place to wander about and meet school friends. Each time they went to the park they met more people they knew. Or was that because Lili was getting to know more people? Remember, Megan spoke to everyone, even the animals. She spoke equally to common pets and to exotic zoo creatures — and they seemed to understand. She definitely had a way with animals.

Another summer treat was the bus trip they'd take to a city swimming pool at Hoyt Park where they could cool off and have fun splashing about. Of course, by the time they took the bus back home they needed another cooling off.

Megan with the pretty smile and outgoing friendly way was a natural target for boys. Lili could only glance at them, letting Megan do the talking. Vivacious boys were especially attracted to the pretty Irish girl. Lili often wondered why and was thankful for the way vivacious boys had quiet friends. Quiet Lili often found herself talking with the quiet friends as Megan jabbered on with the outgoing boy.

Don't be mistaken — Megan was not a flirt. She just liked people and they liked her. Whether ice skating, walking in the park, swimming or boating, Megan and Lili would meet other kids — sometimes boys, sometimes girls, sometimes both — enjoy the afternoon and giggle about the boys all the way home.

A few times a year, Megan and Lili boarded the Center Street bus, transferred to the downtown trolley, and went shopping on Milwaukee Avenue. Because of Megan's love of exploration, they found the Mall (in days before super malls). This Mall was a collection of interesting little shops crowded together in the basement and first floor of an office building located between the Boston Store and Gimbels. They entered the Mall by way of an iron spiral staircase, another adventure when they tried it the first time. And oh, the treasures, all kinds of treasures, from popcorn to friendship bracelets. The girls always checked it out during their trips downtown.

These adventurers didn't hesitate (at least Megan didn't) to stroll into very elegant dress or specialty shops. Once Megan pulled Lili into a tiny leather shop. Oh, the musky smell of leather belts, shoes, purses, and luggage. The next time they were downtown, it was Lili who insisted they return to the shop where they both bought pairs of huraches, with real leather straps woven into cool summery shoes (they cost $2.99). All the way home on the bus, they sniffed the leather and gloried in their purchases.

At school Megan and Lili seldom shared classrooms. In fact, the only teacher they shared was Mr. Kolmas in the first half of fifth grade. They did, however, share recesses and after-school activities. They both were Girl Scouts and attended the same Sunday School and church. As Girl Scouts they often used weekend outings to earn badges in skating, boating, hiking, sailing, skiing, tobogganing, cooking, and such. Megan was an artist; she could draw and paint beautiful pictures. Lili was more of a crafts person, preferring to knit, sew, and string necklaces. As Girl Scouts they knit watch caps for servicemen, sewed layettes for the Red Cross, and wrote letters to lonely people serving their country in strange places around the world. Megan, the artist, drew pictures to include in the letters that Lili generally wrote while her friend dictated the message.

Megan sang with a lovely soprano voice; the girls liked to harmonize, Megan with the top notes, Lili with the bottom ones. Because Megan learned new songs quickly, she was the one to teach Lili the latest hits: "Three Itty Fishies", "Don't Sit Under the Apple Tree", "Hutsut Ralson on the Rilla Rah", and "Maresy Doats", for starters. Hoagy Carmichael was one of Megan's favorites; Chopin was another. She knew all the words to "Old Buttermilk Sky" and "Till The End of Time", the latter taken from Chopin's "Polonaise". But Lili's favorite remained Ella Fitzgerald and her jazz tune, "A Tisket a Tasket".

Overnights at Megan's house were the most fun. Lili could get away from her little sister for a few hours; Megan's house offered more privacy. On the other hand, Megan loved to spend nights at Lili's house so she could share that same little sister; she didn't have one of her own. During those nights the girls would fix each others hair, trying to work curls into Megan's thin blond hair and Lili's thick brown hair. They tried bobby pins, sock roll-ups, and wave lotion. Nothing worked. Yet, each time they walked around, hair rolled up, they envisioned the curls soon to tumble about their heads.

They dressed up in their mothers' clothes, whisper into the wee hours, and begin the whispering all over in the morning. They were the times to enjoy the cooking of a different mom and experience the tastes and habits of a different family. Megan's mom cooked spaghetti sauce that simmered all day, and Lili's mother showed off her new recipe for spaetzel she just learned from Mrs. Ludwig. The nights the girls shared were times to lean out the window to call to the nerdy boy who lived next door to Megan, times to play their favorite games, and times to just sit and read together; best friends do that.

Megan was everyone's best friend. She liked the kids that others didn't like, a champion of the nerds and the have-nots. She loved people with her big innocent heart, loved them deep down where it counts. No one loved Megan more than Lili.

Megan's birthday was May 15. The day has never passed without Lili thinking of her friend and remembering all their adventuresome times.

"Till the end of time,
Long as stars are in the blue
Long as there's a spring,
A bird to sing I'll go on loving you.
Till the end of time,
Long as roses bloom in May…"*

[*From Megan's favorite song, "Till the End of Time" by Buddy Kaye and Ted Mossman, based on Chopin's Polonaise, Santly-Joy, Inc., New York, 1945]

The Mural

The World 1939 — Francisco Franco, leader of the rebel forces, wins the Spanish Civil War and takes over the Nationalist Government. Refugees flee to France.
Czechoslovakia, abandoned by British and French Forces by the Munich Treaty, falls to Germany.
Albania is taken over by the German army.

THE CHILDREN KNELT BEFORE THE MURAL, carefully selected colored chalk, and painstakingly filled in the lines. As children do, they focused on their work, giggling occasionally as they paused to pick up another stick of colored chalk. Some of the kids were better at coloring than others, but all were intent on doing their best to please Miss Horne.

Lili had arrived at the school early, dragging her sister Angel and pleading with her to walk bravely into her classroom. "You'd think you'd be done being scared after all these weeks," Lili chided. "See, there's your friend from yesterday, Abby Ethel Epstein." Lili pointed to a little girl with thick glasses. Angel reluctantly let go her sister's hand and walked toward her friend.

Lili got out of there fast, taking the steps to the second floor in rapid hops. She wanted to have time to work on the mural before the bell rang. This was only the second day, but already it was showing its many colors.

"Lili," a young voice called to her. "Wait up." Lili spun around to see her new friend, Anna, climbing the stairs behind her. "Gonna work on the mural?" she grinned as she threw her arm around Lili's waist. Anna was in Miss Horne's class too and lived just a block away from Lili. The two met most mornings on the way to school and shared the walk.

"Are you kidding? Of course I'm going to work on the mural. I've been coloring in the Indian section." The girls knelt down before the brown paper and fished out pieces of colored chalk. "How's your mom?" Lili asked.

"She's better, I think. Daddy went off to work today, so she must be okay. Don't look now, but Guess Who just walked around the corner."

"Anna! Shhh. He'll hear you."

"So?"

Anna and Lili leaned over their work judiciously avoiding looking at the boy who walked by. "Hi Anna, Lili." The girls could tell without looking up that he was smiling.

Anna sat back on her heels and looked Harold straight in the eyes. Lili continued coloring the feathers on the brave's headdress.

"Goot morgen, Harold," Anna greeted him with her best German accent.

"Yah," he accented the word.

"Don't let Miss Horne hear you say that," Anna warned. It was Miss Horne's job to weed out the accents, especially the yahs.

Lili could only give the boy her best smile before returning to coloring the Indian headdress. She could never let this sparkly-eyed boy know how much she… admired… him.

"Old Miss Horne doesn't bother me," he swaggered past them just as Miss Horne came through the classroom door.

"Harold!"

"Yes, Miss Horne."

"Time to take your seat inside." Her face didn't tell him whether or not she had heard his remark. He squeezed past her into the classroom. In a softer voice, the teacher called, "Come on now, Anna, Lili. Time to come inside. You can work on the mural when you finish your arithmetic."

The first days of school had smoothed out and had become routine. Lili discovered music classes and, soon after, she discovered art classes. The other schools she attended hadn't offered art or music; or maybe they were subjects saved for the higher grades. Lili loved the opportunity to listen to music, the chance to sing, and the time to express herself with paints.

Music class was held in the basement music room. The class marched in a line through the hall and down the stairs where another teacher, Miss Richter, played the piano and taught them songs.

"When I play the notes, you sing along," she told them that first day. "Here are the words to the first line: 'I come from Mon-tan-a... I wear a ban-dan-a...'" The class followed as the teacher played. "Now the next line: 'My spurs are of silver, my pony is gray.'" Miss Richter also had a magical Victrola that played records. "We'll listen to operas and symphonies and concertos during the year," she promised. Lili loved every minute of music classes. She had always wanted to be a singer, maybe like Judy Garland who belted out songs and accompanied them with tap dancing. Only Lili decided to forego the dancing.

Soon after fourth grade got underway, the children were invited to choose a musical instrument and join the band or orchestra. Lili chose the violin — it was small enough to carry and didn't look too difficult to play. While her mother fussed over the budget, her father took her to a music store to spend $11 on a violin. The school didn't offer group lessons, so her parents found an instructor who taught her to play the violin on Tuesdays after school. Each week Lili proudly carried the black violin case the many blocks to Miss Myrtle Barr's house. Miss Barr was an elderly woman who brought beautiful music out of Lili's cheap violin. Patiently she directed Lili's fingers and guided her ears until the girl could play a fairly adequate "Twinkle Twinkle Little Star". That's when she got to join the school orchestra, positioned in a back seat right in front of the trumpets. Lili was busy for the rest of that school year with violin lessons, orchestra practice, and everyday learning.

The art class fascinated Lili as much as the music. Never before had Lili done any painting with water colors. All she had at home were crayons and coloring books. She could stay inside the lines very well, but it never occurred to her to draw anything for herself on blank paper. When Miss Horne brought out the brown butcher paper and announced the beginning of the mural, Lili learned she actually had a talent for drawing simple shapes and for using color. Not only did she color "inside the lines", but she added trees and mountains to the background.

For all her shyness, Lili gradually made friends with others in her class. For Lili, "making friends" consisted of learning someone's name and smiling at them occasionally. Lili almost never spoke to someone else first; she waited for them to begin a conversation. Because she was an outsider, Lili felt she didn't belong and, therefore, kept her distance. Megan was an exception — probably because Megan wouldn't take no for an answer. She seemed to sense Lili's loneliness. The caretaking heart of Megan insisted they become friends, and Lili was willing.

By the end of the October, Lili had memorized most of her classmates' names from the roll call list. She learned that Anna Gruber, the girl she walked to school with, came from a German family who still spoke their native German at home. She also singled out Etta Robertson and Minette Hershfield, a twosome who had been best friends since kindergarten; Doreen Johansen, the girl with relatives in Holland; Mary Beth Koubena, whose family had come to Milwaukee recently from Greece; and of course Megan Murphy. Etta, Minette, and Doreen had formed a "Secret Girls Club" they called the SGC sometime back in the second or third grade. Before the year was out, they invited Megan to join them. And Megan insisted they include Lili in the invitation.

Since Megan and Doreen weren't in Miss Horne's class, the SGCs could meet only during recess. During those meetings, the girls huddled in a corner of the playground and giggled at the boys while sharing their darkest secret dreams.

Miss Horne's mural project wasn't planned as an international culture lesson, but it was turning out that way. The students were drawing pictures of children from countries around the world. They painted the children wearing native costumes in their natural settings: the Dutch children wore wooden shoes and baggy pants and picked tulips; the Japanese children wore kimonos and ate with chopsticks; the Chinese children wore tapestry robes and led a colorful twisting dragon; the English children sipped tea while wearing proper jackets and prim dresses. There were Arabs in flowing robes riding camels, Greeks dancing in white skirts, French kids in farm clothes tending vineyards, Swiss yodelers calling out from atop the mountains, Germans in Tyrolean pants herding cows, Italians in bright shirts eating spaghetti, Russians in furry caps dancing with bears, Brazilians in banana headdresses dancing sambas, Mexicans in sombreros and serapes leading donkeys, and American Indians in war paint dancing around an open fire.

When the mural was near completion, Miss Horne led a discussion about the heritage of her students.

"Where are the Jewish kids?" Minette Hershfield asked.

"Jews don't have a country," Miss Horne explained. "Jews have a religion and can live anywhere, like Catholics," she went on.

"Catholics have a country," Etta spoke up. "I think it's called the Vatican."

"You're right, Etta," Miss Horne smiled wanly and continued. "The Vatican is the center of the Church" (she emphasized the capital C), "but Catholic people live all over the world. Catholicism is a religion, just like Judaism."

With the question of religion versus nationality apparently answered, the teacher continued. "We all have parents or grandparents or ancestors who came to America from some other country. That's why we call America the melting pot of the world."

"What about Indians?" one child asked. "Didn't they live here first?"

"You're right, Donovan," Miss Horne returned. "Indians were here when Columbus arrived, so they must be the very first Americans. But they have their own religion too and keep to themselves on reservations. They don't mix with us in public schools, rather like the Catholics."

During the lesson that followed, the children learned several new words: *immigrant, native, heritage, descendent, alien*, and terms such as: *first generation, new arrivals*, and *melting pot*.

The mural was hung in a special place of honor in the hallway next to the school office down on the first floor. The day the children pinned it up, they held a celebration. Pupils throughout the school wore native costumes to school, each depicting their own heritage.

Lili fumed and fussed because she didn't think the French wore distinctive clothes.

"There's no French costume," she wailed, until her mother came up with what she called a "peasant shirt," a full-sleeved blousy shirt. "It's kind of nice," Lili conceded, "but I still wish I had Arabian blood in my family so I could wear a colorful costume — like a desert princess, with full satin trousers, head scarves, and a flowing robe, like Nancy's going to wear."

"Nancy? Arabian?" Her mother appeared awed.

"I guess so."

"Is her skin brown? Her eyes and hair brown?"

"Sort of. Her hair is like mine."

"Oh," her mother said, lowering her eyes and glancing quickly toward her husband, who sat reading his newspaper in the living room.

"Why? Mommy. Why do you ask?"

"Oh, no reason," her mother said through pins held between her lips. She continued to pin up the hem of the peasant skirt. "This will look so pretty on you," she said as the last pin was put in place. "Now slip out of it and I'll do the hem."

Each of the children of Miss Horne's class signed their names across the bottom of the mural, and Angel delighted in pointing out her older sister's name to her second grade friends.

Up on the second floor, Lili was surprised when her classmates remarked about her beautiful French costume. "You look as if you could climb the Eiffel Tower," Harold remarked.

"Really? I look… French?" Lili managed a smile.

"Oh yes, very French."

The school assembly for the children was meant to heighten awareness of One World, shrinking. The school orchestra played some stirring march music; some sixth graders read poems about peace; and the entire audience was excused, one class at a time, to the tune of "Hi-ho, Hi-ho, It's Off to Work We Go", from the new movie "Snow White and the Seven Dwarfs".

For the rest of the day, through the school assembly program, through classroom studies, through recess, Lili felt as if she was walking on air. Harold liked her costume.

The effect on Angel was different. Angel realized she was losing her sister to her second floor friends. Lili now played with Megan or Anna after school. Anna seemed always "there" because she lived closer. On days when Lili played with Anna, the girls rushed home, changed their clothes and met in the alley — their own private playground.

When Lili didn't feel like going all the way over to Megan's, she settled for her neighbor. But as the fourth grade year progressed, Megan and Lili became closer and closer and generally could be found at one or the others house after school.

"Do you like Megan better than me?" Anna once asked Lili.

"Of course not, Anna. You're my friend, my neighbor. We practically live together. Megan lives way over on the other side of Center."

"But you go over there a lot. And she's over at your house a lot too."

"We like each other. Besides, I feel sorry for her; she has no sisters or brothers. She's an only child."

"Oh yeah. I know. Poor Megan." Anna tried to buy the explanation, but she never felt like Best Friends with Lili. "You're just embarrassed when you came to my house because my family speaks German, not English."

"Don't say things like that," Lili told her. "I love to talk to your Grandmother Gruber and hear her speak German." Lili had learned to call her *Grosmutter* and in turn taught the aged woman a few words of English — words such as *history* and *arithmetic*.

Lili also liked to play with Anna's younger brothers and sisters; there were four. These were reasons Lili liked to visit Anna at her home. They were the same reasons that Anna much preferred visiting Lili's house.

"It's so quiet," she told Lili one day. "I like to come here. Your mother doesn't play the radio and your sister doesn't climb all over us."

"Can't you turn off the radio at your house?" Lili asked.

"No, that's how my mother practices her English."

"Do you speak German?"

"Just enough to say hello to my grandmother. My folks want us kids to talk in English."

"I wish we spoke another language," Lili said.

Anna shouted at Lili. "No you don't! It's awful. Nobody understands you, even other Germans who come from other parts of Germany. It's awful; don't ever wish that." Lili could never understand why Anna felt that way about her family.

THE GIRLS OF THE SGC held their meetings intermittently and spontaneously during recess, sometimes on Tuesday, sometimes Thursday, sometimes on Monday. One of the girls would hail the others as they left the building and the meeting would get underway. Once Anna was talking with Lili when the other girls approached, arms around each other, singing.

"Hi, Lili, we're having an SGC meeting. Come on."

"Sorry, Anna, I have to go."

"Can I come too?" Anna asked. "I'd like to join. I know Megan and Etta and…"

Minette cut her short. "We have to go."

The club had drawn its membership lines at five, even though Lili and Megan asked to bring Anna along.

For some reason, the other three girls objected. Lili didn't think much about it until that moment.

When the girls began their meeting, they talked noisily about what had just happened. "Why can't we invite Anna?" Megan insisted. Lili kept quiet, preferring to stay out of the controversy. She thought she knew the problem. Minette was the one objecting the loudest.

"She's not…" Minette began, then retraced her words, "she's too… she's… well, she's German. Can't you hear her accent? She might be a spy or something."

"A Nazi?" Megan put the implication into the word. "You think she's a Nazi?"

Lili couldn't stay quiet any longer. "All Germans aren't Nazis," she offered. "We have German neighbors who hate the Nazis."

"They say they hate the Nazis," Minette came back, "but do they — really?"

The SGCs nearly came to blows over the question of admitting Anna before Megan suggested, "Let's put it to a vote."

Megan and Lili voted to add Anna to their group. Etta sided with her friend Minette, and Doreen followed. After all, her beloved Holland had been invaded by the dreadful Germans too.

There was no room for Anna in the SGC.

The war had begun to touch Lili and her friends.

SHE HAD HEARD THE NEWS that first day of September in 1939 while her family unloaded their furniture and unpacked their household goods in their new home. The radio had carried the account of an invasion into Poland by the German dictator named Hitler. Lili had no idea how important this was until she heard Anna's family discussing it weeks later.

"Are we bad people?" Anna asked her mother.

"Of course not, liebchen," her mother replied. "We aren't the storm troopers who marched into Poland and Holland."

"But they're German. And I heard some kids at school say that because I'm German I'm to blame."

"Don't listen to them, Anna." Lili hugged her friend as her mother stared at her daughter, not knowing how to answer. "Those boys were mouthing off. What do boys know anyway?" Lili tried to console her friend, but she knew what the kids were saying.

Minette, whose family was Jewish, had made the charge during an SGC meeting that the Germans were killing the Jews and were starting a war. While she knew that Anna wasn't to blame, still Anna and her family had come from Germany.

Doreen backed up her friend, telling frightening stories of the German conquest of Holland. "I feel very antsy around any Germans," she told her friends.

"Me too. I'm scared of Anna and of all Germans," Minette replied.

Etta explained that because the Jews and Germans in Europe didn't get along, that had no bearing on how the girls should behave.

She was right of course. But the girls were just children themselves. The war was definitely moving into William T. Sherman Elementary School.

Milwaukee Alleys

LONDON ENGLAND, June 3,1940 — Weary civilian boaters returned from their last trip to Dunkirk. They had saved more than 335,000 soldiers who had been pushed to the sea in France by the Nazi army. There is little hope for more than 30,000 others left behind.

A MILWAUKEE ALLEY IN 1940 had a life all its own. Everybody's alley seemed the same, but everybody's alley had its own characteristics. Lili's alley was just barely wide enough for two narrow cars to pass — very carefully — as long as snow wasn't piled up at the sides. The concrete dipped slightly in the center for drainage and was cracked in many places.

Even though the school with its huge asphalt playground spread out only two blocks away from Lili's house, Milwaukee kids love their alleys. The alley held everything a child needed to play.

During that first autumn in Milwaukee, Lili watched the neighborhood kids who played mostly in their alley playground. In time she learned that the alley was a suitable baseball diamond, racetrack, waterway, skating rink, slide, and hopscotch court. Anyone who has never had an alley to play in may not understand the nature of a real recreation site.

Lili wrote often about the goings-on in the alley. As a Girl Reporter, FC (first class), she made notes she could expand on later. What follows is based on her musings about her Milwaukee alley.

When winter snows began, Milwaukee changed its tune. The narrow streets became silent except for an occasional car crunching quietly over the snow. Fir boughs sagged with heavy snow and sent clumps of the feathery stuff tumbling noiselessly to the ground.

The first snow came drifting down in time for Thanksgiving, sifting white powder over the dry lawns, landing damply on the still-half-warm concrete of the alley. Until one morning Lili woke to find a white blanket across the alley. Two rows of tire marks of an early riser's car ran parallel down the alley. Before many weeks, only chain marks would show in the snow and the rutted ice, making a bumpy surface that would challenge booted feet until spring.

Alleys weren't plowed clear of snow, as streets eventually were. Like the other car owners in the block, Lili's dad shoveled the area behind the garage and adjacent to the backyard. Everyone seemed to know the rules of driveway care; by school time on any given snowy day, the alley was nearly clear. Almost. There were a few places where people either didn't own cars or who were too old to shovel snow. These places waited until some big boy did the work after school.

Weekend snow was dealt with by a different set of rules. On weekends the snow stayed untouched longer to give the kids time to roll snowballs to make snowmen, to build forts and arm themselves with snowball ammunition. The first kids to run outside built the biggest forts. Oh what battles Lili, Anna, and Wilhelm, the boy next door, had with the boys across the alley — the spoiled kid and three of his buddies. During one such battle, one of those buddies put stones in his snowballs and one hit Wilhelm. Lili didn't see the guilty boy around there much after that; she knew Will had a quick temper and could deliver his own justice.

As the snow piled higher, shovelers made brief attempts to clear snow from in front of the garage doors; then they just gave up. A few car owners put away their cars and let the snow accumulate until spring.

Lili's neighbors, the Ludwigs, had no garage — they had no car. They did have Wilhelm, an energetic son in the sixth grade who they put to work shoveling their alley space clear. Will was learning not only the work discipline so favored by Europeans, but he was building muscles too.

The next house down, beyond the Ludwigs, belonged to Old Mrs. Schneider, who was too old to shovel her stretch of alley. She never drove in winter anyway. She lived alone with just a horrible yappy Pekinese dog for company. The neighbor kids said she didn't even bother to look out the back windows until the snow melted. Will always shoveled Mrs. Schneider's alley after he finished his family's space.

Milwaukee has lots of snow from Thanksgiving to Easter and sometimes beyond. By New Year's 1940, snow on the pavement had melted, then froze into layers of ice. By February, alternate thaws and freezing built up the layers until kids couldn't remember there was pavement beneath. Occasionally, the ice would smooth out.

Lili and Angel held hands as they skidded across the slick ice on their way to school, their heavy rubber boots slithering about on the glassy surface, their squeals disappearing in the crisp frozen air as one or the other fell down.

Children could always find games to play all year around in their alley. When partly melted snow turned back to ice, the alley turned into a skating rink. Lili, Angel, and Will donned their skates to attempt to ice skate over the rutted ice. It didn't work, but the ice still was great for sliding. By mid-winter, huge snow banks were piled on both sides of the alley and formed still another play area. The children climbed them, burrowed into them, and hid behind them.

Lili and Angel were still young enough to wear snowsuits, but that first Milwaukee winter Lili graduated into maroon wool pants with a matching coat-like top. She felt very dressed up. On less severe days she could wear just the coat. The problem was that by the time winter wore out, so did the snowsuit. Each Wisconsin winter meant new snowsuits for growing children.

To Lili at nine years old, winter seemed to last forever. By March, when teachers were pinning yellow and red construction paper daffodils and tulips to the cork runners above the chalkboards, Lili moaned at the white ground cover, "Won't you ever go away?"

The senses of a young girl yearning for plant life to return strained to catch each sign of spring; the process was slow. She kicked chunks of ice in the alley as she walked to and from school, sometimes pushing them all the way to the sewers, then grinding them through the grating. She tried to remember what the alley looked like when it was dry, without snow.

Spring-like winds during a January thaw caused the ice in the alley to melt. After sundown the pools of water re-froze, causing worse ruts. The rutted ice and piled-up snow alternately were transformed into the winter Olympics site, an icy playground, the shortcut to anywhere, the hub of activity.

Yet, in April the snow did go away, melting into rivers that rolled and swirled down the center of the alley toward the sewer grates at the corners. A few piles of dirty snow on the north side of the alley held their own well into May.

As the alley turned into a river of melting snow and gullies, hands became red and cold under soggy mittens. Kids sloshed in the streams with heavy winter boots and sent sailing vessels made of orange crate wood and boats made of tree limbs and plain old sticks rushing merrily on the waves down the alley toward the sewers. "Here comes a dandy," someone would call as a special "boat" headed downstream. The more snow that melted, the faster the boats traveled.

Spring winds eventually blew parts of the alleys dry enough to draw hopscotch courts, ply rope for jumping, and start hide-and-seek games. Spring also brought roller skating, Lili's favorite. She was happy to live near the school so she could meet her girlfriends at the playground on weekends and skate over the wide expanse to their hearts' content. Roller skating was done less in the alley with its chipped rough concrete and more on the front sidewalks because of the smoothness. Sometimes the girls would skate for blocks looking for a stretch of new, smooth concrete. They found the very best skating arena in the newly paved parking lot at the side of St. Joseph Hospital, down at the end of 50th Street.

Teachers at Sherman School, like teachers all over the world, observed the traditional March winds and April showers by covering bulletin boards with pictures of kites and umbrellas and flowers. Still, the flowers outside took a bit longer. Then one magical day, just before Memorial Day, the alley was clear, dry, and ready for summer.

The clearing days often coincided with the last days of school when Lili packed up her desk and collected her school papers and books. The papers were no longer white and neat, nor the books pristine; they were wrinkled and creased and soiled and... used. Yet, neither she nor the other students ever wondered why they bothered to carry papers home rather than dump them in a convenient waste paper basket at school.

The books were different. School texts had to be carefully gone through, page by page, with a large art gum eraser to get rid of pencil marks. (The marks were always pencil since the only pens used in elementary school were nubbed pens used during penmanship lessons.) The refurbished books were carefully stacked near the classroom door, ready for collection and recycling for next year's students. Lili carried home her own books — her dictionary, a book of Robert Louis Stevenson poems, and her Girl Scout handbook.

Squinting against the lingering bright sun, Lili could see the leaves unfolding on the trees that faced the alley. Flowers popped out on limbs of fruit trees, promising temptation to those who passed beneath the trees later in the summer — plums, apples, and the lone peach tree in Lili's yard. The peach tree that Lili had found on moving day greeted her in the spring with a gown of sweet-smelling pinkish blossoms.

Alley traffic picked up in the spring. Cars that had been stored through the snow season reappeared. Mrs. Schneider brought her 1938 Buick out for a Sunday drive, putting an official touch to the arrival of spring.

Lili's garage was built for two, but the Rosenbergs in the upstairs duplex had no car. Garage space was narrow and cars had to be nudged carefully in and out. Once the door was closed, there wasn't much room to walk around — if two cars shared the garage. A work bench and cupboard were built-in across the window space at the side opposite the alley door. Lili's dad used the shelves to store gardening equipment. In the end, the garage was useful as both a tool shed and as a play area on rainy days.

These were Lili's favorite days — the spring days. The smell of fresh mud and snow shrank away as shoots of green appeared at the edges of alleys, in the cracks, along sidewalks, around the house. Birds reappeared on the warm breezes, perching on sunny bare limbs as soft green shoots rushed to cover the trees, stirring the world back to life.

In time the murmur of spring turned into a symphony that burst into bloom. The spring of 1940 brought iris, tulips, lilies-of-the-valley, and peonies to the Deveroux yard, and with it the peach blossoms that burst from the tiny tree at the alley fence to promise a bright summer.

Friends in Summer

PARIS, FRANCE, June 9, 1940 — The government of
Norway reported today from London the occupation of
their beloved country by the German army of Adolph
Hitler. Courageous Norwegian troops fought to the
bitter end as the monarchy moved its headquarters
across the North Sea to England. Norway follows the
Balkans — Latvia, Lithuania, Estonia, Bessarabia and
Bukovina. Finland and Denmark capitulated to the
German government earlier this spring. Luxembourg,
Belgium and Holland fell last month. The battle at
Dunkirk, which ended just a few days ago, now
threatens the welfare of France.

BY THE TIME SPRING ARRIVED, Lili had written in her diary
how best friends walk home with one another after
school. Best friends play together at recess and meet on
the return to school after lunch. (Sherman School had no
cafeteria; few schools did.) Lili walked or ran home for
lunch, then returned in time to play for a few minutes
before the bell rang. Feeling less the outsider, Lili played
with her best friends after school — Anna or Megan and
sometimes Etta.

Lili looked forward to another aspect of spring —
doffing the bulky winter clothes. "Muh-ther, do I have to
wear these awful brown cotton things today. I know it's
going to be warm." Those *awful brown cotton things* were
stockings that always stretched out of shape and fell
down. "Yesterday was warm and they're hot and
scratchy."

Then came the day when she heard her mother's joyful words, "Sure, honey, you can wear your knee sox today." That year it was warm enough to change to knee socks in April. By May, Lili was wearing ankle socks.

The end of fourth grade meant bidding goodbye to Miss Horne and the second floor. Lili and her chums had been promoted, kicked upstairs to the fifth grade. With a mixture of reluctance and anticipation, they helped Miss Horne clean the chalkboards, collect and stack the textbooks, remove their proud work from the bulletin boards and walls, and empty the desks. What a walk home Lili had on that bright June day with her collection of pens, pencils, rulers, papers, books, and odds-and-ends thrown carelessly into paper sacks.

"School's out, school's out. Teacher let the fools out," Lili and Megan sang on their way down the alley. How proud Lili felt to belong to a group of friends who could chant together on their way home for the summer vacation, knowing that they'd all meet again in the fall — upstairs on the third floor! The best part was knowing she and Megan had been assigned the same fifth grade teacher, the handsome Mr. Harry Kolmas.

The last day of school had Lili facing her first adventuresome summer in Milwaukee. She had yet to experience the delicious hot days running through a lawn sprinkler, occasional trips with her family to dip her toes into Lake Michigan, the lazy days just walking on the tree-shaded sidewalks between her house and Megan's, lazier days slumped over a new Nancy Drew mystery as she sat under the linden tree in her back yard, and the excitement of getting up before sunrise to take a motor trip across the state to visit relatives at the Fourth of July family picnic.

"We'll be here in the fall, won't we Mom?" Lili asked, holding her breath for the answer.

"Of course, sweetheart."

"Are you sure?" Lili had charged into the house, her face red from roller skating in the alley. She found her mother mending underwear, sitting next to the dining room window where the light was good.

"Well, now, nothing is sure, absolutely sure. But Dad's job is going well and we have a nice house to live in and... and... why? Why do you ask?"

"You know, Mama. Every time I make friends and like where we're living, we move."

"It seems that way, I guess." Rosemary Deveroux looked up from her sewing and stared out the window. "Look, Lili, the peonies are about to bloom. See the little round buds?"

By now, Lili was used to the way her mother reacted to her concerns, which was no reaction at all. *It's as if I'm not even in the room or I ever said anything*, Lili wrote. *I don't care a whit about peonies. I'd just like some clue that we aren't getting ready to move again.*

SUMMER WAS BEST FOR PLAYING GAMES in the alley. Lazy warm days brought more kids outside. Anna came over often and she, Megan, and Lili joined the children for long summer evenings playing hide-and-seek games that covered the entire block. One old ramshackle cottage, three houses down the block, was ringed with heavy shrubbery, making it spooky just to walk past. Dubbed The Haunted House, Lili found that the space under the bushes formed an excellent hiding place to get away from the little kids. When Lili really wanted to hide, she'd crawl back under the limbs and sit still, watching the person who was It pace back and forth trying to work up the nerve to look in the direction of the Haunted House. Only Will ever had that much nerve. In time, Lili and Megan used the natural hiding place to sit and talk — away from the gang, but especially away from little sisters and from motherly ears.

"Do you ever wonder what you'll look like when you're as old as your mother?" Megan asked once as they scrunched into their green hideaway.

"Naw. That's too far away. Do you?"

"Sometimes." Megan took a deep breath and shook a leaf away from her face. "I think I'll be tall, much taller than I am now. And I'll wear my hair in a French twist and I'll wear red lipstick and…"

"I never thought about wearing lipstick. Ooh, wouldn't that be fun. Maybe I'll let my hair grow out too."

"Sometimes I think I'll become a great painter and have my paintings in galleries all over the world." Megan looked into space, her paintings framed and decorating the walls of some great museum.

"I think… I think I'll be a… secretary." Lili squinted her eyes, then reconsidered. "No, I'll be a… teacher!"

"Are you kidding?"

"No. For real. I'll probably be a teacher."

"After you win the Olympics figure skating medal?"

"Or the medal for running." Lili wiggled back into the bushes, letting a branch half cover her face.

"… or after you write your book?"

"Well," Lili began, "maybe I can do it all. But Mama says I need a career to fall back on. Figure skating, running, and writing are okay to think about... now... but she says a woman needs a career... just in case her husband dies."

"I'm not going to have a husband."

"Ever?"

"Never! I don't need one. I have me. And I'll have my paintings."

The girls sat still then, their eyes half closed as they tried to see into the future.

Summer was the time for vendors to ply their trades through the alleys. Farmers in horse-drawn carts brought fresh fruit and vegetables throughout the summer. "Strawawawawber-rees," the plaintive voice called out. Clear from the next block, the sound of "Strawawawawber-rees, get your red, ripe strawawawawber-rees" would send Lili's mother scurrying to look for change. "Stop him," she'd shout from the window. "I want to get some strawberries; I have to find my purse." Then Lili and Megan would go to the fence and watch as the old horse lumbered through the alley towards them. Usually by the time it arrived, Lili's mom, still wearing her apron, was there with her money. The girls helped her look over the produce and choose the box with the biggest juiciest berries.

Another familiar alley traveler in a horse-drawn wagon was the ragman. His old sway-back nag clip-clopped down the alley as the man sang out, "Rags today, anybody got rags today? Rags!" The cart was always piled high with old clothes. Nobody ever seemed to know what happened to them. Perhaps this was a kind of clothes recycling business. Or maybe the cloth was melted down and used to make paper. Lili and Megan thought it fun to watch the old driver and horse and conjure stories about where they came from and where they went with their wagon piled high with colorful pieces of old clothing.

"I'll bet he pulls his wagon down to the river and dumps all those rags in to wash them," suggested Lili.

"Naw! Too much work. He takes his horse, Dobbin, and drives down to the poor section of Milwaukee and gives the clothes to the misfortuned," said Megan in her self-assured tone that Lili believed.

"Really? But why?"

"Because the misfortuned need clothes. They don't have money to buy them."

"We don't buy clothes," Lili said softly. "Are we misfortuned?"

"Where do you get your dresses?" Megan asked.

"Mom makes them. She makes all our clothes, except our shoes."

"Well, you see? The misfortuned don't even have money for shoes. Making clothes is different than buying them. You still have to buy the material." Megan hurriedly offered more explanation to avoid insulting her friend. "My mama doesn't sew, and she can't make clothes for me. And sometimes her friends give her clothes for me. But we aren't misfortuned either. We buy our own shoes." Megan narrowed her eyes, looking beyond Lili's shoulder, then added, "Except once. Somebody gave me some white sandals. I wore them last summer, but they got too small." Then she shut up.

The two girls sat for a while under the peach tree as the lumbering horse pulled the rag-filled wagon past them and off down the alley, the man still calling, "Rags, rags, anybody got rags?"

Alley trade traffic began in June with the sound of "spring asparagus" and "strawberries" the early arrivals, followed in season by "raspberries" and "tomatos" and then "sweet corn" and "watermelon", before the autumn "pumpkins and apples". All summer long, to the delight of children who ran alongside and the housewives looking for a special supper treat, the fresh vegetables and fruit wagons rumbled down the alley.

Horses were regular sights in the city, causing no great flurry of excitement when they appeared, nor much notice of anything except a few fresh "horse-apples" in the alley after they left. (Mr. Ludwig would grab Will and run out to the alley with a shovel to scoop up the treasured fertilizer for his rose and tomato garden.)

Regular trades people who generally delivered from the streets during the snow season moved their routes to the alleys in summer — the milkman, newspaper deliverer, grocery delivery boy. By 1940, some of them were thinking about exchanging their horses for delivery trucks. A few already had.

You'll Have 27 Children

WASHINGTON, DC, June 22, 1940 — President Franklin Roosevelt has pledged help for the ailing Great Britain, now threatened with an invasion by the mighty forces of Germany. After the fall of Dunkirk and now the fall of France, the United States fears for the safety of its ally, England. Canadian and American pilots have gone to support the RAF and the home guard efforts of England to defend its shores, and the Merchant Marines are rushing supplies to their British friends.

THE LONG DAYS OF LILI'S SUMMER 1940 brought hit-and-run baseball games, along with marbles and jacks played on shaded concrete. The warm summer offered long breezy auto rides with the family — trips around the city. To the Lake Michigan shoreline. To Washington Park Zoo to rent rowboats, feed the elephants and watch the fun on Monkey Island. To Whitnall Park Gardens to see the glorious roses, marigolds, zinnias and dahlias.

The Deveroux family took its regular summer vacation trip up north for the Fourth of July, spending lazy days playing with cousins, swimming in Lake Pepin on the Mississippi River, hiking the hills that rose from the Mississippi valley, and shooting fireworks in the backyards of relatives' homes. They repeated the visits to northern relatives at Christmas time.

Lili earned spending money by mowing the lawn, cleaning the garage, and straightening the attic. She spent it on movies at the Uptown Theater and treats at the drug store on 52nd and Center with Megan.

Lili's dad offered her the work space in the garage to start a butterfly and insect collection. He helped her carefully set up killing jars, display sheets, cellophane covers and storage boxes. She might have won an award for her neat and careful work, but she came to hate the senseless deaths she was causing and opted instead to enjoy the butterflies and insects as they hummed and buzzed and flitted about the garden. She doesn't remember ever purposefully killing another insect after that, not even mosquitoes (who never seemed to bother her anyway).

For Lili, the summer, free of music lessons and school, took on more life. One of her favorite alley games was hopscotch. She and Megan scratched out the boundaries with a piece of chalk squirreled away from the last days of school or with a chipped stone, using the broken edge to mark the pavement. Each new form was bigger and better than the previous one. Their favorite markers were stones or glass worn smooth by winter snows and rushing spring melt. Lili once had a smooth piece of lucid blue glass — she thought of it as a sapphire. The flat lucky stone lasted nearly two seasons, a long time for a girl whose mother claimed the girl misplaced or broke everything she owned.

Jump rope in the alley was another favorite. Lili's dad had provided some lengths of barn rope that was much better for jumping than clothesline. The heavier barn rope slapped the ground meaningfully and was especially good with double Dutch. Lili and her sister Angel, Anna and Anna's sister Helga, and Megan learned all the litanies:

My boyfriend's name is Marcello
He comes from Pocatello
With a big red nose and a pimple on his nose
And that's the way the story goes.

and

I love coffee; I love tea
I love the boys and the boys love me.
How many children will I have? 1...2...3...
Who will I marry? A...B...C...

They giggled, especially when Lili's foot tripped up on "H" (Harold Hoffman's initials), or on the special initials of the boy who had caught Megan's eye at the time. And they howled with laughter when the number of children rose into the 20s and 30s (because the girls were good jumpers). "You're going to have 27 children and you're going to marry Harold Hoffman," Megan squealed as she sprawled on the grass.

"Am not," Lili insisted, trying to keep from laughing. "I'm going to have 28, you miscounted," and then both girls rolled in the grass until they could laugh no more.

Jumping rope as a group meant having at least three people, two rope turners and a jumper or two. This isn't always easy without an alley. But any action in the alley always brought out more people to play. Often, Lili and Angel tied one end of the rope to the fence and began their chanting and jumping. Before long, out popped Anna or Helga, or maybe even Wilhelm (who liked to jump the rope but didn't like to do the turning).

"You took too long a turn at jumping," someone complained.

"Hey, it's my turn now."

"You said 'just one more.' That's it. You're finished."

And if the jumper didn't take over the turning, the rope was simply dropped onto the pavement. Then the disgruntled turner had to be cajoled back into play before the game could continue.

SHAGGING STONES was an alley game that nearly cost Lili her eyesight that summer. Wilhelm loved baseball and could usually be snared into a game if there were a couple other neighborhood kids in the alley. Since he and Lili were the oldest, they usually got the game going. All they needed was a pitcher, a catcher and a batter. Well, maybe a fielder if there were four kids around.

One afternoon in late June, Lili was at bat and Wilhelm in the outfield. Anna was trying her best to throw the ball where Lili could hit it, and Angel was competing with a neighbor boy to catch it. As Angel chased after still another errant ball, Will, bored at the slow pace of the game, started to shag stones down the alley. As he spun a stone into the air, it took a nasty turn and headed straight toward the batter, striking Lili just above her eyebrow. Lili screamed her pain as Will rushed up, whipped off his shirt and tied it around her head. He led the wounded Lili, bleeding profusely, into her kitchen as he repeated, over and over, "I'm sorry, I'm sorry. I didn't mean to hit anyone."

Lili's mom, used to handling the crises of childhood, calmly washed the bloody gash and applied a gauze square, stemming the blood flow by tightly covering it with adhesive tape. "We'll have the doctor look at it after your dad comes home," she told Lili, who by then had stopped crying and was becoming angry.

"He could have killed me, Mom," she howled, waving her arm dramatically.

"Now now, it's a deep wound, but not life threatening."

However, the doctor leaned more towards Lili's appraisal. That evening, after Lili's dad had taken a look at his wounded daughter, he called the doctor, who came right over. "A bit close; more blood than damage," intoned the doctor as he stitched up the gash. "But a few centimeters closer and you'd be peering out of one eye, young lady."

Actually, Lili and Will got along rather well, sharing responsibility as the older children. Both were the oldest in their families. Yet, tempers flared on occasion. Once the two were "discussing" the fairness of a homerun when Lili got so mad she slugged Wilhelm right in the eye, bringing on the shiner that drew respect for Lili from the entire neighborhood, respect both for Will's black eye and for Lili's aggressive fist. For the time being, the two warriors were even.

Will's family was German at a time when their homeland was causing a stir in Europe. Their thick accents and strange phrasing, along with blue-eyed, blond appearance, identified their heritage in a city composed of first- and second-generation middle Europeans. Will's little sister Francine, with a chubby angelic face framed in blond curls, and their new baby brother Holt remained untouched by the hysteria aimed at Germans in Milwaukee in the early 1940s. But Will was beginning to catch some of it.

"Does my father love Hitler?" he asked his mother one day after a classmate had cornered him on the playground.

"What happened?" his mother returned.

"He pushed me up against the fence and said that Father was a Hitler-lover," he told his mother. "I asked him, 'Who's Hitler?' and he held me while he told me."

"Vat did he say?" asked his mother, not wanting to hear the answer.

"He said, 'You know, heinie, he's the guy who is trampling all over the little people in Europe. Don't you know Shikelgruber, Adolph, the Nazi with the little mustache? Come on, you're German. He comes from your country.' Does he? Does Father love Hitler?" The boy looked to his mother for some answer to the madness. If he had heard his parents talk about this before, he hadn't paid attention. After the playground encounter, he began to listen more closely.

"He's mad if he tinks he can invade England," he heard his father say one evening. "Chasing dem into de Channel vas one ting, but going de stream across, dat's another."

"Are we related to Hitler?" Will asked his father later.

"Such a question," the older man scoffed. "You tink we're related to dat mad man? Ach, liebchen, who gave you dat idea? Who have you been listening to?"

"Ah, nobody," Will lied. "I just wondered."

"Vy vould you vonder dat?" his father pressed on, trying to get Will to open up.

"Well, we're Germans, aren't we? Are we Nazis?"

"Nein, nein," Will's father shook his head and left the explaining to his wife.

"Nein, Will," his mother said. "All Germans are not Nazis. In fact, dat's vy ve left Germany ven you vere little. Your father didn't like da vay people vere following Hitler, ain'so, Papa?" she nodded at her husband. "So, ven your uncle Fritz said he vas leaving for America, ve decided to come too. You see? Ve ran *away* from Hitler. Ve're not related."

Will's mother and Lili's mother had become good friends, the over-the-back-fence variety. After the Monday morning race to get the laundry on the line, the two women often paused, dropped their wash baskets to the ground, and leaned their elbows on the fence to gossip.

Lili's mother, a simple woman raised in the isolation of a northern Wisconsin farm, was a paragon of justice and humanity as she carefully developed friendships with all her neighbors. She fed her children large doses of anti-prejudice lectures, meaning to equip them with tolerance for others. She and Mrs. Ludwig saw eye-to-eye on that subject, although they never agreed on whether pancakes (blintzes) should be rolled up or served folded.

Lili remembered her mother's admonitions about life in the big city, delivered before the move to Milwaukee. "Things will be different there, noisy, busy, crowded. You'll have to learn to get along with a lot of other kinds of people."

"What other kinds of people are there, Mom?" Lili asked one day after school.

"People who were raised different from you, who may even look different. I hear tell of people who have black skin, some with brown and… even yellow skin. You'll see all kinds of those people. And you have to remember that it's only the skin that's different. We're all alike underneath."

"You forgot red."

"What?"

"You forgot red skin. Like the Indians. They have red skin. You forgot to say that."

"I… ah well, I… didn't mean… well… of course… red. Yes, some people have reddish skin."

Lili caught a strange look on her mother's face, but thought no more about it. She looked and looked along Milwaukee streets as she became more familiar with the city, but she never saw any people of those different colors that her mother had described.

The family that lived on the second floor above the Deverouxs was German too, but seemed not as young or as well off as the Ludwigs. Mr. Rosenberg had three small children who didn't live with him, but came to visit a few times. Lili's mother often sent up a casserole, a pie, and outgrown clothing for the children, but never once did Mr. Rosenberg or his mother come downstairs to visit.

"MAMA, MAMA, GUESS WHAT?" Lili rushed into the kitchen where her mother was preparing dinner. The midsummer heat had brought out Mama's recipes for cool macaroni and pea salad.

"Slow down and catch your breath."

"Guess, Mama, guess," the excited girl wouldn't be slowed down.

"I give up," her mother said, shelling the fresh garden peas into a bowl.

"I have a new friend. And guess what, she's a grownup. Like you. Only she isn't like you. She's..." Lili caught the look on her mother's face and stopped short. "She's... ah... she's not a mother."

"You mean she has no children?"

"Yes. She says she can't. But she has other things."

"Really?"

"She has a washing machine that automatically squeezes out the water and there's a clothes dryer. And she has a wonderful garden and she let me run her vacuum cleaner..."

"Really!" Rosemary Deveroux saw her opponent clearly through her daughter's words. "She... lets you run her vacuum cleaner?"

"Oh yes. After we finished the luncheon dishes, she pulled it out and let me do the living room. Oh, did I forget? She fed me lunch. That's why I wasn't here. And she showed me how to do needlepoint and we listened to her radio and..."

"Well, you seem to have had a very busy day. Did she let you do the laundry too?"

"No, Mother, this isn't even laundry day. But she showed me the washer and dryer."

Lili's mother did the traditional Monday laundry in the basement using an old washing machine with an electric motor-driven plunger and wringer. She heated water on an old gas stove in a large copper kettle, pouring the hot water into the washing machine and the rinse tubs. Clean clothes were fed through a rubber roller wringer between rinses and carried up to the backyard clothesline to dry. After several loads of wash, the machine and tubs were emptied into the basement drain.

The process usually took Rosemary Deveroux most of Monday mornings. After a brief lunch rest, she would begin to reclaim the dry clothes from the line. When clothes became too dry, she had to "sprinkle" them with tap water from a sprinkler bottle.

Tuesdays were ironing days. Since a conscientious housewife ironed almost every piece of clothing, bed linen, and underclothes, the task took up much of the day. Rosemary couldn't stop thinking about her daughter's new friend who seemed to have easier ways to handle the family laundry.

"And you did the dishes? I hope you didn't wear her down too much with your grumbling."

"I didn't grumble," Lili answered, slowly realizing how she sounded to her weary mother. "I mean, there weren't many dishes. Okay, I'll do them here without grumbling."

"Where does your new friend live? And what is her name?" her mother changed the subject.

"Grace. Her name is Grace Martin and her husband is Earl and they let me call them by their first names." Lili had never called a grownup by a first name before.

"Don't you think..."

"No, Mother. She said it was all right. And they live just two houses down the street."

"You were that close and didn't hear me call at lunch time?"

"Oh, sorry, no, I didn't hear. But we were so busy, we just sorta sat down and had a snack and then..."

"I know. Washed the dishes. What's this about needlepoint?"

"Grace does needlepoint. She'll teach you too if you want. She let me do a few stitches on her piece, and gave me a piece of my own to work on. It's fun."

Lili's mother didn't spend much time doing needlepoint. Once Lili had found her embroidering some pillowcases for a friend's wedding, but Rosemary Deveroux had her work days planned ahead. She had even embroidered the tasks on kitchen towels during the early days of her marriage: wash on Monday, iron on Tuesday, mend on Wednesday, shop on Thursday, clean on Friday, bake on Saturday, pray on Sunday.

Mothering seems so confining, Lili wrote in her diary. *I hope I never become a housewife. It's almost like slavery. Mother never has time for herself. She's always keeping house, washing dishes, cleaning and stuff. She told me today that I ought to plan to have a career. I'm not sure just what I can do for a career, but Mama says it beats housekeeping. I think she'd like me to be a secretary or something, like Rosalind Russell in My Favorite Secretary.*

But mostly Grace Martin just listened to Lili's dreams. And as the friendship grew and Lili could see how it affected her mother, she offered fewer details at home about Grace. In a way, Lili was afraid her mother would become jealous of the neighbor and send her to live with the Martins. Hadn't she jokingly threatened to do that a few times? Maybe she wasn't joking. Lili had heard many stories about parents during the Great Depression who had given away children because they couldn't afford to keep them. And now British children were being sent away to keep them safe from bombs. While Lili loved to spend time with the Martins, she loved her family more and would never want to move away.

Not wanting to take chances, Lili limited her trips down the alley to Grace's house to two or three times a week. On those days she'd come early enough in the afternoon for tea cookies and a session of needlepoint. Before the end of summer, she had completed a small scene that Earl helped her frame for a birthday present for Rosemary.

On the hottest summer days, the alley became the place for hoses and sprinklers and children in bathing suits. Hose fights broke out between hastily-formed teams and everybody became refreshingly wet. The best day was when Lili and Will set up a sprinkler in the alley for the afternoon. Just when the little children began to wear out, the sound of "Watermelon. Melon. Watermelon" came droning down from the head of the alley, accompanied by the clippity-clop of the horse. Will dashed indoors to his mother and Lili went to call hers. They each came through with a quarter, enough to give the kids a special treat.

At summer's end, the jump rope was looped over nails on the garage wall, the hopscotch marks faded, and hoses were put away as new school clothes appeared and children prepared for the trip back to school. By September, alleys were clear during the days except for horse-drawn wagons offering sweet corn, apples and pumpkins.

Blessed are the children who have big old alleys to call playgrounds. Too bad that so many suburban homes reduced play areas to a driveway with a basketball hoop nailed to the garage!

Fifth Graders
Move Upstairs

WASHINGTON, DC, September 10, 1940 – Franklin D. Roosevelt, now campaigning for election to an unprecedented third term as President, has announced the United States is sending destroyers to aid Great Britain in its struggle against the forces of Adolph Hitler. London, bombarded since June, is weary from the onslaught and welcomes all help from the USA. Meanwhile, Mussolini's Italian forces have advanced through Libya and into Egypt in an effort to control the Mediterranean Sea.

DON'T TELL MY MOTHER, but I'm ready to go back to school," Lili whispered to her friend Megan one day in August as they strolled along the shady street eating ice cream cones.

"Me too. Won't it be dreamy moving up to the third floor. We'll be in fifth grade!" Megan waved her cone in the air as she twirled around.

Fifth grade turned out to be everything they hoped. First, Lili and Megan were in the same class. Secondly, they had the dashing Mr. Kolmas for a teacher. The only speck in Lili's life was that Harold had been assigned another classroom.

The kids at William T. Sherman already knew about Rosh Hashanah, Yom Kippur, Jewish New Year, and Hanukkah. Non-Jews struggled to control their envy of the Jewish kids who observed the fall holidays by staying home from school. Lili wanted to learn more about the strange holidays celebrated by her friend Minette. During an SGC meeting, Minette explained all about the upcoming holidays, her audience listening to the Old Testament Bible stories as if for the first time.

Megan and Lili often mused about who was Jewish and who wasn't. They had learned of the clash between Germans and Jews, but they weren't sure why. "Maybe if we know who is Jewish, we'll know why," Megan offered one afternoon as they walked home from school.

"Do you think Harold is?" Lili asked. "Mom says Hoffman is a German name."

"It's hard to tell," Megan replied. "Most of the Jewish people here come from Germany and have German names. My mama says Germans and Jews are the same thing."

"But that's not what that crazy Schickelgruber rants and raves about," Lili said. "You've seen the pictures at the movies, the stupid little man with the black mustache and the hair in his eyes. He says that Aryans are better than Jews...."

"What's Aryans?" Megan interrupted.

"I'm not sure. I think it has something to do with blond hair and blue eyes."

"And that's supposed to be better?" Megan never could understand shortcomings. She wasn't at all patient with people who couldn't appreciate others for who they are. She was just one of those natural *People* people.

Both girls had noticed the growing war tension at the movies. The newsreels seemed to be filled with news of this country or that country falling before the German boot of Hitler or Italy's Benito Mussolini. A few pictures slipped into the newsreels of Germans harassing Jews, who were made to wear large yellow stars of David. But mostly the photos were of the devastation of London from the German bombs falling on it.

That 1940 autumn, Megan and Lili saw a new movie called "Heidi" at the Uptown Theater, a movie made from Lili's favorite book. The girls were allowed to go to the movies alone twice a month, that is, if they could save up the dime it cost for admission. They loved the drama of the adventure and always managed to find their dimes, plus another dime for treats at the soda fountain next door.

Some of the movies they saw mentioned the fear that was growing throughout Europe about the German aggression. But the 10-year-old Lili and Megan weren't paying much attention. There were more pressing issues facing them. Another winter was fast approaching and outdoor playtime was short.

In school, Mr. Kolmas introduced his class to choral speaking and started them off with "Hiawatha". First he asked everyone to memorize the poem. Then he showed them how to speak together, directing them just like he was leading an orchestra. Lili loved it and kept practicing at home.

One evening while she was sing-songing her way through the many verses, trying to keep them straight in her head, her father walked in carrying an open magazine and stared at her.

"What are you doing?" he asked, his face ashen.

"I'm memorizing 'Hiawatha'," she answered.

"Where did you hear that?" he asked.

"In school. We have to memorize it for school."

George Deveroux put down his magazine. Was this the time? He wasn't sure. "Let me hear you — from the start," he said finally, sitting down on the bed.

"By the shores of Gitche Gumee," she began. When she finished the last of the many verses, he hugged her warmly, murmuring, "Good job," picked up his magazine, and quietly left the room. For a moment, Lili was puzzled. But only for a moment. Soon she returned to practice the rough spots that needed more work.

Lili was the first to be able to recite the entire poem for Mr. Kolmas. "That's very good, Lili," he told her. "You almost look like Hiawatha as he talked to the stars." The teacher placed her in the middle of the chorus so that she could lead those with faulty memories.

After school in the fall, the frantic pre-snowfall fervor kept children playing long past the early sunsets — red rover-red rover, tag, you're It, hide and seek, and one more game of baseball before the World Series began. Chill winds brought out sweaters and jackets, which were often left draped over alley fences after a strenuous game of red rover.

Lili's special joy came in running. She imagined she was Hiawatha running through the forest, the wind pressing against her face and her swift legs leading her along the path. She could run all the way to Mr. Perlman's grocery store on Center Street without stopping, and she could run almost to Sherman Park if she rested a couple times.

THE OFFICIAL END OF THE FALL ALLEY SEASON came on Trick or Treat night when children en masse donned outlandish costumes and roamed the neighborhood looking for Halloween treats.

Living in small towns, Lili hadn't known about Halloween celebrations. The year before, her first in Milwaukee, she and Angel had dressed up as a ghost and hobo, in sheets and torn shirts made from some of their dad's old clothes. They shyly joined the neighborhood kids, towing their grocery sacks and pillow cases, and started knocking on neighborhood doors, yelling "Trick or Treat, smell my feet, give me something good to eat," then giggling as they waited for the treats.

Megan had joined her friend and the neighborhood gang as they moved noisily through the street: Anna and her sister, Will and Francine, and Lili with Angel.

First they hit each others families, the Ludwigs, Grubers, and Deverouxs. As they toured the neighborhood, their bags began to fill with small pieces of candy, fruit, a lot of candy corn, an occasional penny, and popcorn balls. When they hit the Martins, who had no children, and old Mrs. Schneider, whose children were grown and gone, they received doubles portions of fruit, cookies, and candy. Then… and then… the test.

Lili and Megan stuck close to Angel as they dared their friends to approach The Haunted House, the small cottage set toward the back of the lot covered with trees and thick bushes where Lili and Megan liked to hide during Hide and Seek.

"I'm not afraid," shouted Anna in an attempt to out-do Megan in the bravery department. "I'm not afraid," she repeated as she boldly adjusted her skull and cross-bones mask and tugged at the tattered sheet about her shoulders.

"No don't," her sister Helga called. "It's too dangerous."

"Don't," echoed Lili.

"I fear nothing!" Anna returned and strode toward the small light at the side of the door. Lili, Angel, Megan, Helga, Will, and Francine peered around the shrubbery as she knocked on the door. The creaking sound almost turned them all away, but they kept their eyes glued to Anna who held out her hand and shouted, "Trick or treat, smell my feet, give me something good to eat."

The entire trembling ensemble couldn't believe their ears when they heard a bellowing laugh that tumbled down the walk, past the bushes, and out into the street. "Ho ho ho! Aren't you something! You're a brave one. Here, here's a handful of candied apples for you and your friends. I'm sure there are more of you out there in the bushes. But wait…"

The giant man cupped his hands around his mouth and shouted, "Come on. Come get your treats, you scared little rabbits. My wife and I have made wonderful taffy apples for you, and this little lady is the first one brave enough to come claim hers. Come on now. Hurry. I can't stand here all night."

Lili led the trail of youngsters who peeked through the hedge and slowly walked up the sidewalk to face the owner of the great laugh and the candied apples. As he handed out the treats, he patted each one on the head, saying, "I watch you playing in the alley. You look like such fine energetic children. I wish you'd stop by more often to visit us. Our children are grown and we so miss them."

His wife, a jolly plumpish woman, reached for a photograph and told the children, "Our son is in the Army Air Corps, see his picture there? And the blue star in the window?" Then she echoed her husband's invitation, "Please come visit us when you can."

"Yeah," said Will. "We'll drop in sometime." The others just nodded and thanked the man for the treats. Lili never remembered any of the children ever going to visit the friendly giant who lived with his jolly wife in The Haunted House. A few months later, the children noticed the gold star that replaced the blue one in the window. They heard that the couple's son had been killed in a bombing raid in London.

Bombs showered the British capital city for three months that autumn of 1940. With the Nazis marching through western Europe, the world feared they would soon invade the British Isles. Movietone News at the Uptown Theater was filled with pictures of the staunch heroic Brits as they filed in and out of bomb shelters, sent their children into the countryside for safety, and fought the flames that nearly devoured the great city.

Roddy McDowall, a young British actor, had taken Hollywood by storm and was featured in many films as the child who survived the horrendous London bombings and caught the attention of a faltering America. However much that America supported the British in their plight, they kept most of their troops at home.

Lili's winter brought about school orchestra concerts, a trip up north at Christmastime to visit relatives, ice skating by moonlight on her new white figure skates, and presents that still were marked from Santa Claus (for Angel's benefit). Lili had stumbled across two pairs of woolen gloves in her mother's dresser drawer just before Christmas. She received the same gloves on Christmas morning, wrapped in fancy paper with a note from "Santa". She already suspected the Santa game, but now she had proof. Still, for Angel's sake (and because she netted more presents that way), Lili continued to talk enthusiastically about Santa Claus for a couple more years, as much for herself as for Angel.

Saturday night family games at home were another Deveroux custom. Since Saturday was sure to be the one night when George Deveroux would be home, that was the time chosen to indulge the head of the family in his hobby. Lili's dad made games for his kids — board games, wooden paddle games, the kinds of things he found in *Popular Mechanics* magazines.

His woodworking shop in the basement held all kinds of tools with which he fashioned toys and gifts for his family. When Lili had nothing better to do, she'd follow her dad downstairs and "let" him show her how to use the tools at his workbench. About the only thing she had tried to make was a sailboat, last winter. She had painted it silver and then forgot all about it, even when the spring thaw brought rivers for fine sailing gushing through the alley.

IN THE FIFTH GRADE AND ON THE THIRD FLOOR that autumn, Lili felt the responsibility as one of the older students who confidently walk the halls of the school. The big kids felt like they owned the place.

"I have Miss Nicoud," Lili squealed to her friend Megan as she looked at her report card after the holidays. The beginning of a new year also heralded the beginning of a new term at W. T. Sherman Elementary. With two terms per school year, students often moved to different classrooms mid-term. But not all of them.

"Oh no!" Megan cried. "Oh no! I'm not moving. I stay with Mr. Kolmas. We won't be together."

"Ohhh," moaned Lili. Then she brightened, "but we'll be right next door.

Miracle of miracles, Harold also was moved into the class taught by the wonderful Miss Mary Nicoud. Lili noticed that the teacher often brought her knitting to school and worked on it during recess. Once Lili brought hers to school and they worked together.

"I'm making a watchcap for a sailor," she told her teacher.

"You're doing a good job too," the teacher answered.

"I love the small yarn you use. Isn't it hard to knit with such fine yarn?"

"No, you get used to it. When I finish, I'll give you the extra yarn and let you make something with it, maybe a doll dress."

"Oh, I don't play with dolls, Miss Nicoud," Lili objected.

"But you must dress them up and set them on shelves. Some people make fine collections of such dolls. Perhaps you could start your own collection."

"Well, yes, I do have a few dolls." Then she added, "But I never play with them... I guess I could make clothes for them, maybe costumes from different countries."

"A fine idea. Here let me help you untangle your yarn." Miss Nicoud leaned over and picked up the ball of yarn that had rolled under her desk. When she handed it back to Lili after winding it up, she noticed Lili's fingers.

"What's wrong with your hands?" she asked innocently.

"Nothing." Lili turned her hands back and forth. "Nothing. Why?"

"Oh, I noticed your fingernails are gone."

Lili felt like hiding her hands behind her. She drooped her head and quietly explained, "I… I bite my nails… sometimes… not always… sometimes." Her voice trailed off weakly.

"But you have such lovely hands. Don't you realize that? Look at those long fingers. That's right, you play the violin, don't you?"

"Yes, and the piano. Do you really think they're pretty?"

"Yes I do. Very pretty. And how much prettier they'd be if you let your nails grow. You could even polish them."

"I don't know… if I can…"

"Of course you can, if you want to. Anyone who uses their hands as much as you must have polish on her nails. You knit, you write, you play the violin and piano."

Within a month, Lili had kicked her nail biting habit. In two months, the nails began to grow out. If the beautiful Miss Nicoud wanted her to grow lovely nails, she would. After all, weren't they fellow French women together?

Actually, Lili's French ancestors did not come from Europe, as Miss Nicoud's had. At least not as recently. They came from Canada. Grandparents from both sides of Lili's family traced their childhoods to Canada. There was a bit of Irish in there too on her mother's side, but her father's name was French and that made her French.

In the early days of the war in Europe, Miss Nicoud and Lili followed the tragedy of the French people, vicariously sharing their grief at the loss of their country. Lili practiced spelling her name with a small d and a capital V (as in deVeroux) and other variations, like endings of eaux or ot. She insisted her friends pronounce her name Lill-lee, with the accent on the second syllable, like Lilí Marlene. She once considered changing her name to Muiguette, the French word for Lili.

Miss Nicoud's remark about making costumes for dolls set Lili to thinking. And when Megan showed Lili a doll she had made out of cloth and cotton batting, the girls set off on a new project together.

MEGAN HAD JUST COMPLETED a Southern Belle, which had black piglet curls and wore a hoop skirt of blue taffeta, remnants of a gown Megan's grandmother had worn. "I think the idea of making dolls is swell," she told her friend. "We can find all kinds of material to make costumes. Come on, let's do it."

"My mom's got bags and bags of cloth in her sewing room," Lili offered. "But. I'm not great with sewing needles. I'd rather knit."

"I'll teach you. We can get doll forms down at the Ben Franklin — that's where I got Melanie, my southern belle. I have another, but I haven't dressed her yet. We could make a huge collection if you'll help."

"I'm not sure…"

"Come on, Lil, it'll be fun. Let's start drawing up some designs now. Then we can get the dolls and start sewing. And you can even knit something for them."

The day had turned rainy and the girls had finished their homework. Neither was ready to end the day, so the idea fit the bill. "Oh, all right. Could I make an Indian princess? My mom will show me how. She has beads from when she was a Campfire Girl. I saw them in her drawer once."

"Natch. My next one will be a Dutch girl. I may even decide to make wooden shoes."

"Oh, I could do that," Lili offered. "I've made things out of wood with my dad."

Over the next few months, Megan made dolls and Lili dressed them. They chose figures from the fourth grade mural as their models. Although the mural had long ago disappeared, the girls recalled the costumes that each figure wore and began to create dolls to match them. Very shortly they had turned out a dozen or so dolls, some dressed in colorful international costumes.

As the war droned on, they added four female military dolls to their collection, a WAC, a WAVE, a Marine and a WAF. They were the most proud of the details of the insignias on each of the uniforms, painted carefully with ink and a fine-point pen.

"WHEN WILL THE WAR END, DADDY?" Lili climbed up next to her father in his big chair.

"Not sure, honey," he said, half folding his newspaper and putting an arm around his daughter. "Technically we're not even in the war, although we support what England is doing."

"It seems as if we are."

"I know. But there are many bad people out there threatening the world, even the United States, with their ideas." The father was trying to soft pedal the news that was daily causing him more and more concern. He didn't want his daughter frightened; yet he thought she should be aware of what was going on.

"How much do you know about the war, Lili?"

"Just that people are being bombed and Hitler is killing people and big tanks are running into other people's countries, like Norway and Denmark and the little countries — Latvia, Lithuania and Estonia..."

"You know names of those countries?"

"Yes, our teacher talked about it one day when the Nazis tore through them last spring. Mr. Kolmas thinks that he might have to go into the Army if our country gets into the war."

"Well, that could happen, now that Holland and France have fallen."

"You mean, if America declares war, the men will have to fight, just like in Europe?" Lili's tummy gave a flip as she considered the chance her father would have to go to war. Quietly, she asked, "Will you have to go... to war?"

"Let's just wait and see what happens. We aren't in the war yet, but it may not be long."

And it wasn't. With the fall of France after the battle of Dunkirk, the fear of actual invasion of the Nazis into England loomed like a shadowy monster. What would it take to stop the German hordes?

President Roosevelt was re-elected to an unprecedented third term of office with his promise of aid to Great Britain. By the first of 1941, United States industry had geared up for war, turning out battleships, fighter planes and bombers, tanks and transport vehicles, weapons, equipment, and food.

"Here, sweetheart, read it for yourself." Lili's father handed her the newspaper, opening a whole new world of information and ideas to his young daughter. After all, if she were going to be the world's greatest Girl Reporter it certainly wouldn't hurt to learn how other reporters wrote.

Throughout the rest of that year, Lili joined her father each evening to read the newspaper, check out the maps, read the stories of heroism and tragedy that daily made up the front page. She followed the German army as it invaded the great country of Russia, the Italian armies as they moved into Yugoslavia and Greece and then into North Africa.

Late in the fifth grade she couldn't resist writing a report about the "Diaper Revolution" in Yugoslavia. Intrigued by the movies that told of the heroism of people in the conquered countries, Lili had heard about the boy King Peter II of Yugoslavia. In March 1941, she read how the government, under Peter's uncle, had yielded to the demands of the Nazi troops against the will of the people. The children rallied behind their young king and overthrew the government that betrayed them and prepared to fight the Nazis themselves.

On March 25, boys and girls, aged 10, 11, and 12, let off steam with typical Balkan gusto, staging sit-down strikes and rioting. The grammar school students tore Hitler's pictures to shreds and denounced the traitors of their own government. Slogans deriding the weakness of the government were scrawled in childish handwriting on walls and doors as thousands of hungry youngsters barricaded themselves in their schoolhouses and refused to obey orders from anyone.

Belgrade was never more proud of its young than on those days in March when the young said things the whole city wanted to say, but didn't dare. Truth coming from children made a great impression. The newspaper stories that Lili read explained that the children were repeating what they had heard at home, which showed clearly how the country felt. "They're just trying to throw out the people who wanted to hand their country to Hitler and Mussolini," Lili wrote in her essay.

Miss Nicoud gave Lili's essay an A and a note that said, "Very good work, Lili." Nevertheless, ten days later, the brave little country of Yugoslavia fell to the Axis forces.

Soon after, another Mediterranean tragedy struck closer to Lili. She and Megan had finished the Dutch, Irish, French, and English dolls and were working on the Russian and Greek dolls in late spring when the war shook their friend, Mary Beth Koubena.

Mary Beth, Lili's classmate in Miss Nicoud's room, was a dark-haired girl whose parents both came from Greece. While the fall of France had not directly involved the dramatic Lili in Europe's tragedy, Mary Beth's family story of their escape from Greece did.

The strong Greek people had refused to yield to the storms from Germany and Italy. They rallied under their King Paul, then threw out the government that betrayed them and prepared for a long fight against Nazi tyranny. However, after many weeks of intense fighting, Athens fell on Sunday, April 27, 1941, their king fled to South Africa, and the hated swastika flag of Germany was raised over the Acropolis. Mary Beth didn't come to school the next day.

Harold, Harold, Marvelous Harold:
(Great Romances of 1941)

MOSCOW, RUSSIA, June 22, 1941 — German troops stomped across the Balkans and turned toward Leningrad, the Ukraine, and the Black Sea.

HAROLD HOFFMAN AND LILI spoke very little to each other. She watched him from a distance, followed him around the playground, stole peeks at him during class and managed to stand near him in lines more often than anyone else noticed.

Harold was an outgoing boy who made friends easily; Lili was a shy girl who was drawn to his shining brown eyes. Their only contact in fourth grade was the seating arrangement that put them next to each other on the first day. During the first half of fifth grade, Harold was placed in another room, and Lili had to follow Harold long distance.

Then came mid-year and Miss Nicoud's room.

"Guess what, Megan," Lili was panting as she caught up to her friend on the playground. The January day in 1941 had turned sunny and, while the air was still very cold, the sun's unexpected warmth boosted spirits.

"What?" Megan answered, barely missing a beat skipping rope. She had found a spot on the pavement that poked up clear between ice ruts. The feet of many children kept the snow and ice from piling up on the playground, and a friendly janitor occasionally took out a shovel to clear the play area. Today the sun was helping to melt off more of the ice.

"Guess who is sitting in the next row, two seats ahead of me."

"You got Miss Nicoud, right?"

"Yes. You know that. I'm sorry you didn't move too."

"Yeah, well I just love Mr. Kolmas. He's so dreamy. I think he's better looking even than Clark Gable."

"I'd say he was even better looking than John Payne."

"Oh yes, I saw him with Alice Faye in 'Hello, Frisco, Hello.'" She sang the last few words to the beat of her skip rope. "So, Lili, what's your big news?"

"Oh, almost forgot. No I didn't. Wait till you hear…"

"Well come on, Lil, spill. What's the news?" Megan stopped the rope and sidled up to Lili.

"Guess who's sitting in the…"

"I heard all that. I give up. Who is sitting in the next row, two seats up?" Megan was losing patience.

"Him. Harold Hoffman!" Lili waited for Megan to swoon. Like she did over Clark Gable.

But Megan only answered, "Lili, what's the use of mooning over Harold when you won't even speak to him. There he is, over by the fence. Go over and talk to him… now," Megan turned and pointed to the group of boys slapping each other on their backs to keep warm.

"Oh I couldn't, Megan. I just couldn't."

"Why not? He won't bite."

"Yes he will, I mean, I know that. It's just…"

"Just nothing. Come on, I'll go with you." Megan tugged at Lili's hand, pulling off her mitten as she did.

Lili took the chance to hang back. "No, not now. I'll have to get up the nerve."

"And when will that be? When you've graduated from high school and he's gone off to college? Come on. Now."

But Lili wouldn't budge. "I'd rather not, Megan, if you don't mind," she said very quietly. "Maybe tomorrow. I'll try to get up the nerve… tomorrow."

"All I can say is, what good is it being in class with Harold sitting across the aisle if you won't talk to him? He might as well be in… in… Norway."

The practical odds were against close friendship between Harold and Lili. Harold didn't play in the orchestra; Harold no longer sat on her side of the room once Miss Nicoud moved a few people around; Harold didn't like to draw. Harold liked to play baseball at recess; Harold liked to run and yell with his friends; and Harold disappeared in the opposite direction after school. In short, Harold and Lili seldom found each other in the same place, except back in the fourth grade, when both had become safety cadets. Even then they shared the same duty corners only twice.

Still, Lili adored Harold, or at least the idea of him. She confided to Megan that she thought he was the best looking boy in class and the most popular. She sent him a valentine, making sure it was a comic one. Both Lili and

Megan agreed that he probably was the most inaccessible to Lili.

Particularly after Laura Lanville moved in.

Laura entered the lives of Miss Nicoud's fifth grade class a couple weeks after mid-year. As if the winter wasn't dragging on long enough and cold enough to make Lili miserable, here came interference in the form of a pretty fifth grade interloper.

Laura obviously came from a rich family since she wore expensive store-bought dresses and had her hair curled every day, by a hairdresser, according to Megan.

"Nobody could have hair that curly naturally!" Megan had sided with her friend soon after Laura's arrival. "I'll bet she even puts face cream on at night, like her mother or her big sister!"

Laura sauntered into Miss Nicoud's class on a Monday morning and was assigned a seat directly across the aisle from Harold. Lili saw the writing on the wall immediately as she watched how he offered to help with Laura's books, Laura's papers, Laura's pencils, even Laura's sweater — reminding Lili of how he had helped Lili herself on her first day. Come on, Harold, don't make such a jerk of yourself, she silently warned him across the room.

At recess, Harold offered to show Laura the playground, much like he had shown Lili. At lunch, Harold and Laura walked home together across the northwest corner. Lili traveled the southeast corner home.

"Darn! I mean, drat!" she told Megan when they met on the playground after lunch the next day. "They even live near each other."

"How's that for chutzpah?" Megan agreed. She loved using Yiddish words she learned from Minette. "Look at them mooning over each other. What a pain."

"She's got cheek, all right," Lili agreed, not taking her eyes off her silent swain and his new conquest. Harold and Laura walked slowly from the northwest corner toward the school building, looking at each other and nearly bumping into the fence. Harold paused to extend his hand to Laura as they climbed onto the playground through the bars of the fence.

Harold was as smitten with Laura as Lili was smitten with Harold, an observance clear to just about everyone except Harold, Laura, and Lili. But Lili didn't give up.

Before the story can continue, there are a few things necessary to know about how things were in Milwaukee in 1941.

TELEPHONES WERE FAIRLY NEW just before the war. City phones came with options that allowed users either "unlimited" service or "two-outgoing-calls-a-day". Since Lili's family didn't use the phone much, her parents had chosen the limited service. They could make more than the limited calls, of course, but at a cost of five cents extra for each call. And while that sounds infinitesimal looking backward, Lili's mother considered it substantial enough to discourage extra calls. After all, the Great Depression was still fresh in her memory.

Lili decided to call Harold, and she knew she had to plot carefully. Either she could wait for a day when she knew her mother hadn't used up the allotted two calls, or she could choose an opportunity when she was babysitting at the home of a family who had unlimited telephone service. She chose the latter.

Lili sat with Minette's little sister and brother on alternate Friday nights when Minette's family took her to Temple services. A couple weeks after Laura Lanville had hit the scene, Lili looked up Harold Hoffman's number in the phone book, discovered they both had phones on the KIlbourn exchange, and memorized the number so she would be ready when the next Friday came along.

That night she made sure the children were tucked in their beds and the house was quiet before she approached the telephone. Lili sat down next to it about eight-thirty and stared at the machine for a few minutes. She tried to imagine what she would say, how Harold would answer. *How will I sound? What reason will I give for calling him?* she wondered.

Homework, a work assignment. "Didn't Miss Nicoud ask us to look up something?" She couldn't remember. Probably not.

A whim. "I thought I'd just call up and chat." No, nobody just called up somebody to chat. Not in 1941. And certainly not Lili; she wasn't the chatting kind.

A question? Yes, a question that no one could answer except Harold Hoffman. Of course! "What is your address? I want to send you an invitation to..." But Lili never sent invitations. Would Harold know?

Perhaps she ought to ask about... but she had little in common with Harold except her attraction to him.

Lili continued to stare at the dial, wondering what reason she could give for calling on the telephone. She checked on the sleeping children. She stood at the window and watched cars drive by. She walked into the kitchen and drew a glass of water and sipped it slowly before returning to the telephone. She just wanted to talk to him, to hear his voice. She continued to stare at the telephone.

That's it. I'll call, wait for him to say Hello, then hang up. I don't have to speak. But would he know it was me? He might. Lili dialed the number carefully. Somewhere in the night, along dark cables, a connection was made and the ringing began. The phone rang the coded two short rings — once, twice, three times, again, and again. Lili's heart pounded. How long should she let it ring?

Finally an interruption. Someone picked up the receiver. Her heart stopped pounding; her heart stopped… period. Her breathing stopped. She heard a very sleepy "Hello" from a male voice, a fatherly voice. She gulped, gasped a mouthful of air, and asked carefully, "Is Harold home?"

"What?" asked the surprised voice. "Of course Harold is home. He's sleeping."

"Oh," Lili exhaled into the mouthpiece. "Oh," she repeated.

"Who is this?" the voice asked. "Do you know what time it is? Who is this?"

"I'm sorry," she whispered pathetically.

"It's almost midnight," the voice came back angrily. "Are you some kind of spy? You know I work for the war effort… or are you just trying to scare me. You leave my son alone, you…"

But Lili heard no more. "Oh," and she repeated "oh," and hastily hung up the receiver. She glanced at the clock. Ten minutes before midnight. No wonder the voice was sleepy. She had let hours pass struggling with her decision. *Oh, I hope they don't know who I am. Oh me! How will I ever face Harold again?*

But she did, and often. Now that she had made a contact with his private home life, he became a real living person to her instead of a fantasy. In the months that passed, she learned that he lived just a couple blocks from her house. She took the opportunity to walk past the house (on the opposite side of the street), hoping to see him, and afraid she might. She never caught even a glimpse of Harold... or his family.

Then Laura Lanville slipped out of their lives as abruptly as she had invaded. Her parents moved back East somewhere, Lili heard, just after the start of summer vacation.

Lili managed to approach Harold more comfortably after that, even starting conversations at times and listening to him answer questions she made up. They became almost-friends, somewhere between mere acquaintance and actual friendship.

LATER THAT SPRING, Lili contracted a case of mumps, the most embarrassing disease of the lot of children's ailments. The doctor came to the house and then the Health Department — nailing up a sign that forbade any unauthorized person to enter the home until the quarantine was lifted. For what seemed an eternity, she lay alone in her sickroom, watching children outside playing in the near-summer sunshine. Her parents allowed Angel to remain in their shared room, hoping she would catch the germs and get it over with at the same time. However, Angel never suffered the indignity of mumps.

Quarantine meant that Lili could not go out. One visitor who was allowed to come in was an adult friend of Lili's mother from out of town. When she learned Lili was quarantined with mumps, she brought a bouquet of sweet peas, the first time Lili had ever received a gift of flowers.

"You look just like my mother," Lili's father told her one evening as he came to see how she felt. He sat down on the bed next to her and smoothed her straight dark hair with his hand.

"Really?" Lili asked. "Wait a sec. Grandma Deveroux's hair isn't dark. Her hair is light brown."

"No, I meant my mother. Your Grandma Deveroux is my step-mother."

"You never told me that."

"I'm sure I did — you just…"

"No, Daddy. You never told me Grandma wasn't your mother."

George Deveroux was silent as Lili squirmed under the sheet and sat up in bed. "Tell me about her — your mother. Do I really look like her?"

George took a deep breath. "Sorta," he said at last.

Lili caught what she described later to Megan as "a really weird look" on her dad's face. "He just looked at me and looked and looked," she told her friend.

"Maybe you look more like her than he said," Megan suggested.

"Could be. But there's something else. Maybe I'll ask Mom."

As the pain of her aching throat receded into long boring days of recuperation, Lili smuggled word out to her friends through Angel to come visit at the back window, which was set low on the first floor facing the back yard. Minette and Etta stopped by to visit, as did Mary Beth, talking to Lili as she hung over the windowsill. But it was Megan who came every day to bring Lili up to date about the goings on at school, especially the goings on of the fabulous Harold.

ON HER ELEVENTH BIRTHDAY, Lili received her first Girl Scout uniform. Never before had she owned a store-bought dress. Now she owned a dark green uniform with special pockets and special buttons and a belt with a fancy buckle and a bright yellow scarf that tied around her collar.

The box it came in was bigger than any present she ever remembered receiving, but the contents made her dizzy. Her own uniform. But she had to wait for school to begin in the fall to wear it.

The first chance she got was a Monday. She carefully put on the uniform, adjusted the belt, tied the scarf... just right, according to regulations (Lili looked it up in her Scout manual), and marched off to school. She knew that only a few other girls wore Girl Scout uniforms, and she felt spectacular. Would Harold notice? Not likely. She knew Miss Nicoud would notice, but would Harold? Lili wasn't sure.

Alas, Harold was absent from school that day.

"Just my luck," Lili moaned. "Well, maybe he'll be around to see me next Monday when I wear my uniform again."

"You look spiffy, Lil," Anna said. "He's sure missing something."

After school, Lili found Megan, and the two of them walked the few blocks to the Methodist church for the Girl Scout meeting. "Hey, doesn't Lili look great in her new uniform?" called one of the girls as they entered. The troop leader, Mrs. Gruenberg, agreed and had Lili model the uniform for the other troop members.

Dare to Swim, Lili!

*THE WORLD AT WAR, July, 1941 — German troops
reach the Dniepr River; Hitler orders SS general to
submit a plan "for carrying out the desired final solution
of the Jewish question". FDR orders seizure of all
Japanese assets in the U.S.*

MEGAN'S CHARM WAS WORKING ON LILI. In that summer of
1941, Lili turned from a shy ten-year-old to a curious,
adventuresome eleven-year-old. Not only had Lili dared
to learn the bus and trolley system that took her
downtown, but she was willing to follow Megan along
unfamiliar bus routes to the swimming pool at Hoyt
Park.

"It's one thing to learn the way to the downtown
department stores," her mother had warned, "but quite
another to go someplace that your parents have never
taken you."

"Mom," Lili begged. "Megan's been there dozens of
times. She won't let me get lost. Besides, you always tell
me that a person can't get lost, that they just aren't where
they want to be."

Her mother had laughed then as she gave Lili money
for the bus.

"Can't I go too?" Angel whined, hugging her
mother's hips. "Why can't I go too? I always have to stay
home."

Suspecting that her mother's pause meant she was considering Angel's plea, Lili spoke up, "No, Mommy, we want to go by ourselves, please, huh?"

"Sorry, Angel, but this time it's just Lili and Megan. Maybe they'll take you swimming another day, won't you, girls," she smiled sweetly at her daughter.

"Of course, Angel," Lili smiled just as sweetly at her younger sister, generous with her promises for later.

"We're off," shouted Megan, grabbing up her swim bag and hustling Lili out the door. Outside she whispered, "If we had stayed another minute, we'd have company. You know your mother was weakening."

"Yes, I know. I hate to leave Angel, but not today. We have other things to do." She winked at Megan who returned the wink with a knowing grin.

"Things to do," Megan echoed as they danced out the door singing, "We're off to see the Wizard…."

Lili and Megan had planned the trip for days, deciding on Hoyt Pool since that's where most of their classmates went to swim. It was an outdoor pool at a park that was a considerable distance from Sherman School — at least by eleven-year-old standards. They took the Burleigh bus and transferred only once. "Gee, I hope I can remember the way," Lili said. "I might have to bring Angel here next week."

"You'll be all right. Just remember where we transferred. Besides, I'll probably go with you… if you want me to."

"Of course I want you to. Just going with Angel isn't half as much fun as having you there."

"You remember our plan for today?" Megan coached.

"Not really. I mean, do we have to...?"

"It won't hurt. You're not breaking a law or spending money. You're just meeting boys."

"But we'll be in our swimsuits," Lili moaned.

"So will they," Megan laughed.

The bus ride seemed short and soon the girls were inside the pool house, changing into their suits and checking their clothes and towels at the counter. They walked slowly toward the pool as they tucked their hair inside their bathing caps.

"Oh look, there's the SGC!" Megan elbowed Lili and waved at three girls bobbing about in the shallow end of the pool. They rushed to the edge.

"Hi, Lili, hi, Megan," the bobbing heads called from the water.

"Hi SGC," Megan splashed her foot in the water. The SGC, remember, stood for Single Girls Club, the group that lent its members a sense of belonging (and therefore, self confidence).

"Call the meeting to order, Megan," Etta Robertson shouted.

"Yea," Minette Hershfield added.

"Okay, then, I call the meeting of the Single Girls Club to order," Megan intoned judiciously. "We'll dispense with the minutes today because we don't have paper and pencil to write underwater." She and Lili had advanced to the pool steps.

"Come on in, girls," shouted Doreen Johansen. "It's just swell in here."

"Feels cold." Lili paused at the top step.

"Don't be a fish," Doreen shouted back. "Just jump in. It isn't cold once you're in."

"I've heard that before," Lili told her, then began to lower herself into the water, shivering as she sloshed water over her arms.

"Here I come," Megan shouted before she jumped in, barely missing Minette.

Minette was the best swimmer. She excelled at so many things. Her dark hair and eyes always twinkled when she was doing something well. Minette wasn't one to sit quietly in the corner. Even in school, she was the one who needed to go to the board or fix the window shade or walk over to the desk to borrow a book. In the swimming pool, she continued to tread water as her friends gathered for their meeting, even though the water was shallow enough to stand up.

Etta had to go into much deeper water before she could tread water. Tall for her age, she was always the one in the back row for class pictures, always the first in the gym class line (where girls lined up according to height). Etta and Minette were best friends and were seldom seen without the other. Where Etta went, Minette also went. Except to Temple. Minette went to Jewish Temple Friday nights. Etta went to Episcopal Church services on Sundays. And Etta's hair was as light as Minette's was dark, and her eyes were "cool blue", according to Min.

"Mutt and Jeff" is what many of their friends called them. Etta was tall and Minette was short, kind of a mini-Etta, some said. And both of them loved to be daffy. How Doreen came to join the club is still a mystery. Doreen was... well, I guess you'd want to call her... proper. Doreen always wore proper pleated skirts and jumpers, as well as proper saddle shoes or sandals. Megan described her best as looking like a magazine advertisement. "She looks just like the girls in the Sears catalog," she said once. "Never a hair out of place."

That day at Hoyt Pool, not only was Doreen's hair out of place (it was sticking to her face), she didn't look like an advertisement. As Lili slipped into the pool — up to her neck — Doreen was being dunked by a group of boys.

"Help me," she gurgled as she came up for air. "Help me," she pleaded to her friends.

"Go, Megan," Lili pushed at her friend. "You can make them stop."

Megan half swam, half waded over to Doreen, who was now kicking back and waving her arms in the air. When the boys saw help arriving, they retreated, swimming to the deep end of the pool.

"You all right?" Megan asked Doreen.

"Sure, I'm okay, I just wanted to scare them off. That's that horrible Richard Kamp from sixth grade. He's always making trouble. I sure hope he's not going to Steuben or we'll have to put up with him when we get there next year."

"Who are the others?"

"One is his brother. I don't know who the third guy is. Never mind them, let's get back to our SGC meeting."

"All in favor of sticking together and not paying boys any attention, say aye," Etta announced as Doreen and Megan returned.

"Aye, aye," the girls cheered.

They paddled and giggled and splashed water and tried coordinating their arms and legs to actually swim. Lili maneuvered rather well by keeping one toe touching the bottom.

Megan liked to push away from the side and paddle her arms and legs as fast as she could until she sank. Etta could float on her back and occasionally made a kind of swimming stroke. Doreen preferred to simply move her arms in unison, keeping both feet on the bottom of the pool. Only Minette actually had solved the mystery of keeping afloat by kicking her feet and rotating her arms in unison.

After an hour or so of water fun (the boys didn't bother them anymore), the SGC climbed out and sat on the warm cement, just in time to see three other classmates coming out of the poolhouse.

"Oh, there's Arthur," Etta called, waving towards the boys.

"And James... and... who's that other boy?"

"That's Duwayne, from fourth grade. I think he lives near James." Megan seemed to know everyone.

"Oh, and there's Stanley, the schnook who keeps making me laugh in class," Etta pointed at the fourth boy.

"Hey, do I see some sixth grade girls over there," Stanley said in an overloud voice. "Seems they've been waiting for us."

Stanley was a kidder. He was always getting the girls to laugh by making faces when the teacher wasn't looking. All the girls liked Stanley, even if his front teeth stuck out when he smiled.

Arthur and James lived near each other and both were interested in baseball. Usually James was pitching balls for Arthur to hit, and both were becoming very good. Arthur was the more forward of the pair, making up for James' shyness. That day, though, both boys seemed happy to see the girls from their class.

"Maybe Arthur will show you how to swim," Megan nudged Lili.

"Oh, no, I couldn't. Keep your voice down." Lili pretended not to hear Megan's suggestion. But Megan wouldn't quit.

"Arthur! Oh Arthur, you know how to swim, don't you?"

"Yep, course I do," the boy answered.

"Do you think you could teach Lili?"

"Well… er… uh, Lili, want to learn to swim?"

Lili glared at Megan, but she stood up and followed Arthur back into the pool. The whole group then returned to the water and spent another hour or so splashing and dunking and pretending to swim.

Duwayne found an inflated ball and they started a kind of wild water volleyball. Except no one knew the rules, and they just bounced the ball around the water.

Lili didn't learn to swim, but she thanked Arthur for trying. "There, you see," Megan teased when they were toweling themselves dry in the poolhouse. "You see, you actually talked to a boy and you didn't melt."

"I talk to boys."

"When? I never see you."

"I do. Sometimes."

"You won't talk to Harold."

"Meee-gaaan," Lili whined. "You know I can't talk to Him." The one secret she never shared with Megan was the night she called Harold on the telephone and spoke, very briefly, with his father.

"Well, someday. Someday you'll find out that boys don't bite. They only look like they might."

"You rather like boys, don't you," Lili asked.

"Sure. There's nothing wrong with them."

"Do you have a special one?"

"Uhhh," Megan stopped to think. "Uhhh, nope. I like them all."

"Oh Meee-gaaan!"

The group all boarded the same bus back towards Burleigh. At the transfer point, Megan and Lili said their goodbyes to their friends who took a different bus toward Center Street. The girls snuggled into the back of the bus and exchanged stories about the day at the pool all the way to their stop.

"Could you imagine today if we had taken Angel?" Lili asked as they neared her house.

"Sure. Those guys would love her. You might consider taking her along as... as..."

"Bait? Is that the word you're looking for?"

"Yes. As a matter of fact, bait is exactly the right word. Next time we'll try it. See what we can catch with Angel as bait."

"Megan, you're impossible. See you tomorrow."

Then came September and the sixth grade.

Sherman School Plunges Into War

CAIRO EGYPT, January, 1941 – Egyptian armies have pushed back the invading troops of Italy's Mussolini, but not before they claimed Somaliland and Libya. Field Marshall Rommel has control of the Great Sahara Desert.

SPRING, SUMMER, AND FALL OF 1941 repeated the wonders of Milwaukee that Lili had already discovered. The peach tree that blossomed in the spring bore a tree full of sweet rosy peaches by fall. Throughout the summer the alley remained the center of play and Lili was making many more friends — children with names and nationalities that encouraged new cultural experiences on one hand and conflict on the other.

By the time she entered the prestigious sixth grade, she found herself in a class with a teacher she quickly learned to hate. She had to find her fun as a regular member of the school orchestra, a prestigious safety cadet, a loyal Girl Scout, and a member of the church Junior Choir.

Just before Halloween, teachers came up with another all-nationality day as they did back in Miss Horne's fourth grade. In the fall of 1941 there was a different emphasis. More auditorium programs and more international celebrations sought to honor the many countries that were disappearing under Hitler's boot —

Holland, Norway, France, Greece, Poland, Czechoslovakia, Estonia-Latvia-Lithuania, Rumania, Albania…. After all, many of the students were children of families that had escaped those countries.

All this meant Lili had to come up with another costume. Lili dug out her French peasant blouse, which was in fashion by then. As she straightened the beret, she felt sad to think her beloved France was under siege.

"I look like a hussy," she told her mother. "Don't the French wear anything else?"

"I think you look lovely in that."

"The skirt is too small; I've grown, or hadn't you noticed. I won't go to school next Tuesday. I'll just stay home."

"You'll do no such thing," Rosemary Deveroux told her daughter. "We'll work something out… to reflect your heritage. Or you could quit growing," she added with a smile.

"Mom, am I adopted?"

"Where did that come from? Of course not. Whatever gave you that idea?"

"I don't know. Angel, I guess. She has blond curly hair and mine is straight and dark."

"That's the way you were born. It doesn't mean you're adopted."

"But aren't kids supposed to look like their parents?"

"Yes, and you look like your dad. You have his eyes and his dark hair and sometimes you stand just the way he does, sorta slouching."

"But his hair isn't straight like mine. His is curly."

"You have his eyes and his slouch. Isn't that enough?"

"Daddy says I look like his mother — his real mother." Lili spoke the words quickly and waited to see her mother's response.

"He told you that?" Rosemary's eyes stared at her daughter as her brain scrambled to come up with the right words.

"Yeah, do I? Look like her?"

Rosemary Deveroux closed her eyes a moment. As she opened them, she reached out her arms to her older daughter, wrapped her inside and held her tightly. "You're beautiful," she said. "And you look just like you. That should be enough."

"But do I? Really? What was her name? Did you know her? What happened to her?"

"My, my, my, so many questions," her mother said, standing up. Her eyes had turned on again as she gently pushed her Lili out of the kitchen. "Go get washed up and set the table for supper," she said.

"But..."

"But nothing. Your questions will wait until your dad wants you to know."

"Muh-ther!"

"There's really something goofy about this," Lili told Megan the next day as they worked on their dolls. "What does my dad want me to know? And when will he tell me?"

"Maybe your grandmother ran away from your grandpa," suggested Megan the Romantic. "Maybe she had powers and was run out of town. Maybe there was a scandal. Maybe she died when your dad was born." Megan covered her eyes with both hands. "That would be soooo tragic," wailed the Romantic.

"Well, I'm going to find out, if I have to go ask Grandpa."

The girls returned to their sewing and the subject of Lili's grandmother — the real one — was pushed aside. But Lili didn't forget.

Over the weekend Lili tried to squeeze into the French outfit again, then ran crying to her mother. "Please help me find a costume for All Nations Day."

"Come with me." Rosemary Deveroux stood up and Lili followed her into her bedroom. She knelt before the cedar chest at the foot of the bed and pulled open the lid. The sweet cedar aroma wafted towards Lili.

"What's in there?" she asked.

"Things. Things I had when I was a girl, before I met your father. This became my hope chest, where I kept towels and pillowcases I embroidered for my home."

"Oooh, look, Mommy. What's that?"

"Never mind. It's just a pillow I was working on once."

"It's beautiful, Mom. Did you paint that?"

"Yes." Rosemary gently held up the soft velvet square on which was painted a basketful of red roses. "I was going to make a pillow out of it, but I never finished it."

"Mom, I didn't know you were an artist. This is beautiful."

"Let's put it back. That isn't what we're looking for."

"Will you ever finish it?" Lili asked as her mother lovingly folded the velvet and replaced it in the chest.

"Maybe someday. Oh look, I've found what I was looking for." Rosemary pulled out a box, using both hands to make sure nothing fell out, removed the lid and carefully unfolded a dress made of doeskin. She held it up to show the varicolored beads that formed a pattern around the neckline and on the sleeves.

"Oooh," was all Lili could say as she fingered the soft dress. She let out her breath as she gently touched the beaded neckline. "Oh, Mama, it's the most beautiful thing I ever saw. Where did you get it?"

"This was my Campfire Girl dress. Just like you belong to Girl Scouts, I belonged to Campfire Girls."

"But where did you buy this? Who did the beading?"

"Why, I made this, Lili. That's part of the Campfire Girls. And I did the beading."

"All of it?" Lili asked in amazement. "This too? It's so... so... beautiful." Then she remembered the pretty beads she once found in the drawer. "I'll bet it took you forever."

"Not quite. The beading took me weeks. And it's authentic."

"How do you know?"

"I compared it to a dress your grandmother had..." Rosemary Deveroux began, then stopped short. "Never mind," she finished. "Do you want to wear it?"

"But I'm not Indian."

"Apparently no one else in your class is either. Still, Indians were here before anyone else — way back when. They were the first Americans. Now you're an American too. Isn't that what this celebration is all about?"

"I guess. But…"

"No buts. If you want to wear it, I'll take it in a bit for you. I was chubbier than you when I wore this dress."

"Oh, Mama, it's too gorgeous. Too beautiful. Oh thank you."

When Lili appeared at school for the All Nations Day program, she wore a demure one-feather headdress and her mother's hand-beaded moccasins. Actually she carried the moccasins to school and put them on later.

"Hubba-hubba," Megan told her friend as they met in the hallway. "Where did you find that outfit? You make a beautiful Indian princess, even if you're not Indian."

"My mother says we're all Americans. And I'm representing the first ones," Lili said.

"I wish I had thought of that. But where did you get the outfit?"

"My mother. She made it when she was a Campfire Girl."

"I'm green. I mean that two ways — I'm jealous and I'm Irish. And who knows what Irish girls wear?" Megan had settled on a green dirndl skirt and white blouse that had shamrocks sewn onto it. She even wore green spats on her saddle shoes and green bows in her blond hair.

Etta, whose family still had relatives in India wore a beautiful East Indian costume of flowing silk robes and veil that looked exotic with her flashing dark eyes. Minette wore a traditional ornate Russian costume. Anna braided her blond hair and threw her grandmother's German shawl around her shoulders. The dark-eyed Mary Beth wore her father's white dress skirt of the proud and once-mighty Greek Guard.

The boys mostly wore short pants, the tradition in European countries then, some with brightly colored suspenders, some accompanied with lieder-hosen and some with jaunty feathered hats. One boy wore baggy Dutch trousers, wooden shoes and a tiny pillbox hat on his head.

During the afternoon recess break, Lili and Megan, still wearing their costumes, were playing jump rope with Etta and Minette when two boys came by and stopped for a moment. Etta was jumping, holding her swirling sari close; Lili was holding one end of the rope and chanting when she heard one of the boys mutter softly, "Dirty Indians belong on the reservation."

"What?" Megan asked. Lili's mouth had stopped in mid-chant.

"Indians ain't no good. They're lazy and no good and should stay on the reservation." The boys started to move off.

"And where should you have stayed?" Etta mouthed off smartly at their retreating backs. "Aren't you wearing one of those immigrant suits?" One boy turned around.

"Etta, don't…" Lili shouted.

"Sorry, Lili, but I can't let him get away with that." The boys continued to walk away, but Lili's heart had split in two.

"What a dreadful thing to say," Megan comforted her. "And you're not even a real Indian."

WORDS, FLUNG CARELESSLY INTO THE AIR can never be retrieved. Like remnants of long ago planets that float aimlessly through space, forgotten but ever present, words carry the energy of hate, of cruelty, of uncomprehending malice.

Those who fling such words — and those who are disfigured by them — share the evil. Yet, the words always carry a sense they are meant for someone else, spoken by someone else. Hate names, like words of spite tossed out in anger, aren't meant for you; they're somehow attached to someone else. Likewise, names called to one person feel as if they belong to someone else. No one owns hateful words. No one should.

The Sherman School multi-cultural family came from a neighborhood that included, within a few blocks of each other, a Jewish fish market next to Mr. Perlman's Jewish grocery, St. Anne's Catholic church and school across Center Street from a Hebrew school, several German Lutheran churches, numerous Jewish synagogues, a Catholic hospital, and people from around the world. Kids from families that reflected all those backgrounds attended William T. Sherman Elementary School.

The United States had joined the war in Europe through its support of Great Britain shortly after Dunkirk, adding more troops after France fell to the Germans in June 1940. In a multi-cultured town like Milwaukee, frightened whispers grew quickly into angry shouts among the various groups of Europeans newly escaped from the terrors of war.

In Lili's neighborhood, German families tried to keep to themselves, fearing they be mistaken for "the enemy". Jewish families, living in nearby neighborhoods, tried to contain their fear for the safety of loved ones left behind. The rumors coming out of a warring world were frightening.

The tumult of war had hit William T. Sherman Elementary School. As Europe took sides, so did the school playground. Rumors spread like spilled water. Lili and her friends heard the whispers and sometimes repeated them, awe and disbelief echoing in their words.

Did you hear?

Tony, the beloved police officer who protected the children at the street crossing, suddenly was suspected of being a spy for fascist Italy. He, of course, was as American as any of his small charges, and as loyal; still, his family came from Italy.

Did you hear?

A romance was rumored between the beloved Miss Nicoud, who was French, and Mr. Kolmas, who was Jewish. What the kids didn't realize was that Mr. Kolmas had recently been married and Miss Nicoud had a boyfriend who was serving in the Army overseas.

Did you hear?

That girl's mother hoards sugar. Some say she has an entire room filled with sugar bags. Hoarding was something not to be tolerated by patriotic Americans.

Did you hear?

That boy's father told someone how his brother was ferrying B-17s to England, and the brother was shot down the very next day. Somebody talked. You can't be too careful with war secrets.

The most painful war tremors that Lili would come to know came from words she hadn't heard before. The words were whispered, and sometimes shouted, at school, on the playground, in the hallways, on the way to and from school. She could never shake off the pain of hearing her friends — children like her, not yet in their teens — call each other horrible names, names she had never heard before, names she didn't even understand except to know they were hurtful. Somehow she sensed they were repeating things heard at home, much like the children of Yugoslavia did during their revolt.

She watched fights break out between the kids who shared diverse family backgrounds, usually started when a boy bumped another in line. Sometimes a muttered insult accompanied the bump and it ended there. Other times, the bump was returned and fists pounded arms and carried the battle to the playground.

Lili never got over the sting of hearing words like *kike, heinie, Jewboy, Hitler's kid, German-lover, Jew-lover, fascist, Nazi.* The German children were compared to Hitler, Adolph Schickelgruber, the nasty little housepainter with a mustache. Funny songs and tossed insults ridiculed his name and mustache, repeated as if the German children were to blame for the atrocities of Der Fuhrer.

Nazi swastikas, the symbol of German terrorism, tormented the Jewish children as well as the German children, all of whom had a suspicion but little real knowledge of what was happening in Europe. The six-pointed Star of David, a sacred symbol, likewise was used to torment the children who celebrated their special Jewish holidays.

Lili's insides seethed at the words that reflected the adult hatred brewing in other parts of the world. The hateful words directed against Indians had stung her. For a moment she had felt the hatred of others just because she wore an Indian costume. She thought she knew something about what others were feeling. There she was, in the midst of an unreasonable conflict that had nothing to do with her. Although she loathed the Hitler-led madness of Germany, she could find no reason to hate the blond kids at school. And she could find no reason either to hate the Jewish kids. She decided to direct her anger at "the war".

A part of her was filled with the shame that suggested perhaps she did feel some of the hate that came with allowing someone else to choose her feelings for her, to choose her hatreds. After all, she was French and the Germans had brought France to its knees in June 1940.

Most of the Jewish boys attended the New Method Hebrew School, led by Harry Garfinkel, on Center Street after public school hours. When they wore their yarmulkes on Hebrew School days (or tried to hide them in their back pockets), they were taunted with words that ridiculed the religion of their parents, much like the Jews who were being taunted in Europe.

The other half of the fight was the retaliation that the Jewish kids (and some of the others) did to the children who they thought were German, or who appeared to be blond enough to side with the Germans. Children became very good at guessing nationality from a person's skin coloring, their hair, eyes, and their names. Unfortunately, they were wrong much of the time.

Who could tell the difference between a handsome blond Dutch boy who had an angelic face and impeccable manners and his friend, another blond boy who was definitely German. Few noticed that

Scandinavians were as blond as Germans, and their native countries (Norway, Sweden, Finland) fell to the Nazis.

Another classmate, Maurice Hershowitz with his identifiable Jewish name, dropped the "owitz" in junior high and became Maury Hersh, a dark-eyed, dark-skinned friend who wore a great smile and occasionally a yarmulke.

And there was Lili's neighbor, Wilhelm, a fair-haired blue-eyed boy whose parents had come from Germany and who still spoke with heavy accents, whose father loved to raise beautiful flowers and tomatos and whose mother baked mouth-watering strudel that she shared generously with her neighbors.

Labels, Names, and Confused Children

ATHENS, GREECE, May, 1941 – The German invasion of Crete stands as a landmark in the history of airborne warfare. Crete's mountains and poor harbours designate it as a strategic point in the Mediterranean, from which to launch air attacks.

"WHAT A SHAME THAT WE HAVE TO JUDGE PEOPLE by their looks, and label them and call them names if they aren't like us," Lili cried to her mother one afternoon after All Nations Day.

"What's happened, Lili?" her mother asked.

"At school, kids call each other names. If kids have blond hair they're *nasty Germans*. If their hair is dark, they're a… a…," she couldn't bring herself to say the words she had been hearing. "They even tried to call me names because I wore an Indian dress. Don't people realize that what country our parents come from or what clothes we wear don't make one speck of difference?"

The two — daughter and mother — sat deep in thought for a few moments trying to make sense out of something that seemed senseless. Then Rosemary returned to her knitting.

Lili couldn't let go of her restless thoughts. "What a mistake," she repeated after a moment, "to label kids as German just because their hair is blond. Or to call kids

Jews just because they have dark hair. I have dark hair. I could be Jewish or Spanish or Arabic or Greek or Italian or…" she couldn't think of any more. Does hair color really tell where people come from?"

"Of course not," her mother replied, carefully choosing her words. "But most blonds come from northern Europe… "

"That still doesn't explain who is German and who is Norwegian… or Dutch… or…"

"I know, sweetheart. That's the tough part." She wasn't sure how to counsel her daughter about prejudice and suspicion. "I'm pleased with your open mind, Lili, and I hope you keep it open."

"It's just not fair," Lili cried. "Why do we have to have countries anyway?" The two sat with their thoughts for a few moments. Rosemary lowered her eyes and let the yarn and needles rest in her lap.

A few days later, Lili went to look for her mother. She must be in her room, Lili decided, because the door is closed. Then she heard the voices. She moved closer to the door and heard her mother, "You said you'd tell her."

Her father's voice answered, "Not yet. Not now."

"When? It can only get harder."

"It's not that I'm ashamed…"

"Yes you are. You're hiding your own mother to protect Lili…"

"Protect me from what," Lili burst into the room. "What are you trying to protect me from?" She looked both her terror-stricken parents straight in the eye. For a moment, no one spoke. Then George caught the light in his wife's eyes and began "Well, uh…"

"Go on, George. Now seems like a good time." Rosemary's voice had softened and she sat on the bed and folded her hands.

"Well, Lili," George tried again, "there's something that needs to be cleared up." George was not one to go directly to a subject.

Lili didn't speak. The room was silent except for the ticking of the small alarm clock next to the bed.

"You've noticed your hair is darker than Angel's…"

"Am I adopted?" Lili asked again?

"No, you're not adopted," her father assured her. "But your hair is dark… like…"

"Am I Jewish? Really?" she sounded excited. "Do I have dark Jewish hair?"

"Er, Lili, Indians have dark hair too." The voice came from Rosemary. "How would you feel if you were Indian… part-Indian?"

"Indian?" Lili said. "Indians live on reservations. How could I be Indian? They're different, aren't they?" She looked from her mother to her father.

"In a way." Rosemary said. "But many people are part-Indian. Many of the early traders and trappers married Indian women. And some Indian men have married white women."

"Why are you talking about Indians?"

"Uh, you seemed to show an interest in Hiawatha," this from her father. "And you wore your mother's Indian dress last month, remember?"

"Yes, but I'm not Indian. I'm French. Maybe a little bit Irish. Didn't you say that your dad was part-Irish?"

"You know how people inherit traits from their ancestors — their parents, grandparents, and great-grandparents…"

Lili was watching her mother closely as she spoke. Her mom was trying to say something that her dad just couldn't get out.

"We've never told you this before, but we think you're old enough now…"

Before the sentence could be finished, Lili was on her feet. "What are you trying to tell me?"

Rosemary lowered her head and barely spoke the words: "You're part-Indian. Your grandmother was an Indian."

"That's impossible. I've seen Grandma and she's not Indian. Daddy?" She looked anxiously at her father to correct her mother.

"Not this grandma, your real grandma, your dad's real mother. She died before you were born. Grandpa re-married." Then Lili remembered her dad mentioning something about her real grandma.

"You mean Dad is part Indian too?"

"Yes. Of course. His mother was Indian, his father French. He's half-Indian. You're a quarter. Don't you see, that's where you got your dark hair and your brown eyes. That's where…"

But Lili had heard all she could take in. She ran out of the room remembering all she had heard about Indians and trying to realize *I'm an Indian. No good Indian. I'm lazy and dirty and should be on a reservation. Probably will be if anyone finds out. I'll have to make sure no one does. And to think I wore that darned Indian dress to school. How can I ever go back there? This can't be. They're wrong. Both of them. They're wrong; they made it up. I am not Indian.*

The child remembered her mother's words: "I'm pleased with your open mind, Lili, and I hope you can keep it open." They knew. *They knew and they didn't tell me before.* Lili threw herself on the bed and cried herself to sleep.

"Lili," George Deveroux whispered. "Honey, are you awake? It's almost suppertime. Lili?" The father sat next to his daughter on the bed and gently patted her shoulders.

Her mind began to clear as she heard her father's words and turned to face him. Then she remembered. "Is it true? Did you have an Indian mother?"

"Yes," he said simply. "Yes. She was a Chippewa." He watched his daughter's face as she struggled with the truth.

"What was she like?" Lili whispered.

"She was my mother and she meant the world to me. I didn't think of her as Indian. I mean, I didn't see her as an Indian. She was my mother and I loved her."

"But didn't the kids…"

"Oh yes, as I got older I got razzed, but that came later, when I was in high school. When she died, it didn't matter anymore. Not much mattered then. She was gone." He paused as his thoughts meandered through the years. Then he reached out for Lili and brought her face around toward him. "That's why we've worked so hard to help you accept people for who they are, not who their parents… or their grandparents… were or where they came from. That's why…"

"But you never told me."

"We weren't sure you'd understand before. I'm not sure Angel will understand. Whether or not you tell her is up to you, but we prefer to tell her ourselves when we think she's old enough."

"I won't say anything. I won't say anything to anyone." Confused, her mind raced back and forth from the shores of Gitche Gumee to the dirty reservations as she tried to make sense of her new self. Just a few moments ago she was a young French girl growing up among children of many nationalities. Now she was a part-Indian girl, probably the only one at Sherman School, probably the only one in all of Milwaukee!

Everything had changed. Nothing had changed. As she returned to classes, she began to put cultural slights into a new place. She felt more intensely in favor of accepting people as they were, not where they came from.

Now, more than ever, Lili was determined to include her German friend Anna in the SGC. Just before the Thanksgiving break she convinced the others to include Anna. Megan and Mary Beth had often played with Anna when they were at Lili's house. They knew how funny and how creative she could be. Didn't she invent a totally new game of jump rope?

The SGC met briefly during recess one morning and took another vote. Minette and her friend Etta still voted No, but the others prevailed. Anna became the seventh member. She squealed when Lili told her, and she danced around her friend, hugging her, and laughing with her head tossed back. "Thank you, Lili, thank you, thank you…"

"Everyone was happy to vote you in…"

"I know Minette doesn't want me, but believe me, Lili, I'm not against Jews. I like Minette and hope she'll like me."

"She's okay with you joining us. I think she just likes to be different."

Lili continued to choose friends according to who she liked. "We're like the League of Nations now, aren't we," Megan told her one day as they walked home from school. "You're French, I'm Irish, Etta's East-Indian-English, Minette's Jewish, Anna's German, Doreen is Dutch, and Mary Beth is Greek."

Lili was silent for a moment, then she said, "Megan, I'm… not… I mean, I'm…" She couldn't get the words out.

"What? What are you not?"

"It's that, I mean… Megan, I'm Indian."

"Go on. No you're not. You're French. You've always…" Then she saw the look on her friend's face.

"I'm part-Indian. My father's mother was an Indian, a Chippewa." That's all she said. The two girls walked in silence for two more blocks.

At Lili's gate, Megan asked, "You just found out? They just told you? Like that?"

"Yeah. Well sort of. I heard them talking and I couldn't believe it. Until they told me. They said they didn't think I was old enough to know. They weren't hiding anything, they just didn't think I was old enough before."

"Wow! What a blast. What happened?"

"I cried. I cried a lot. I couldn't believe it."

"And you didn't know when you dressed as Hiawatha's girlfriend?"

"No. Didn't have a clue. Do you think I'd have dressed that way if I'd known?"

"Maybe. It's not so bad to be Indian, is it?"

"I didn't think so before. But now, I'm not sure. Remember that day on the playground? Those awful boys?"

"Oh yeah." Megan shrugged her shoulders and added, "But those guys were jerks. Look at it this way. You're more of an American than most of us."

"Oh Megan," Lili threw herself around her friend and began to sob. Megan let her cry until she had no more tears.

When the tears stopped, Lili stood back and said, "I used to think I was adopted, you know, because my hair is dark and I'm so different from my sister."

"But I don't think you're adopted. You look too much like your dad."

"Do I?"

"Yup. Except his hair is curly and yours isn't."

"I think what bothers me most is that they kept this from me all this time. I'm not a kid anymore!"

The girls went inside then, holding hands and smiling. Maybe being part-Indian wasn't so bad after all.

LILI NOTICED THAT SOME JEWISH BOYS had special first names that were different from their school names. Sometime during the early rumblings of war in Europe,

Lili wondered if Harold Hoffman was German... or Jewish? It didn't matter, she just wondered.

"Do you suppose he is Jewish?" Megan asked her friend Minette one day as the two were crossing 51st Street with Lili, on their way home after school.

"I don't know. Why?"

"I just wondered. What's it like? You know, being Jewish?"

"Like being anything. I'm just me."

"I know, Min," said Lili, "but being Jewish is different. I never knew anyone Jewish until I moved to Milwaukee."

"It's just like being... whatever you are... Catholic or Christian or Islamic. What are you?"

Megan looked at Lili who had to pause before answering. She had never been asked that question before. "I'm... well, I'm... Christian, I guess... not Catholic... Mother says Catholics are very different from us. We're also French Canadian, a bit Irish, but not Catholic Irish. Protestant Irish. That's it! That's what I am... Protestant. We go to the Methodist church."

"Me too. We go to the Methodist church too," Megan added.

"Oh wowie," returned Minette, her hand over her mouth. "I never ever knew a Methodist before. This is great! We're all meeting new... uh, kinds... beings... today. I'm Jewish and you two are Methodist."

Megan left them at her corner and Lili and Minette continued their discoveries until they reached the entrance to Lili's alley. They weren't through talking.

"Can you come over to my house, Lili?" Minette asked. "I think my mother is baking matzo today."

"What's matzo?" Lili asked.

"It's a kind of bread. It's so good. Come on. Do you have to ask your mother?"

"Can I call her from your house?"

"Sure." The girls walked faster now, their destination clear. They turned at 49th Street and walked to the fifth house from the corner. "We live upstairs," Minette announced at the door. "Come on up."

As Lili followed her friend up the stairs and into the kitchen, the delicious smell of cooking came to meet her. "Hmmm, something smells good," she said.

Minette's mother met the girls at the door. In her hand she had a small plate on which were perched two small pastries. "Oh, thanks, Mom," Minette cooed. "This is my friend Lili." To Lili, she waved toward the plate and said, "Here, you'll like this. It's Mama's rugelach, and it's the best."

Lili reached for the dainty pasty and popped it into her mouth. She tasted the sweet crust that surrounded a filling of raisins and nuts, a cinnamon treat that reminded her of her own mother's treats after a Saturday of baking pies.

"Yum," was all she could manage with her mouth full of goodness.

A kind of grunting sound from the corner drew Lili's attention. As she turned, she saw a very old woman sitting on a plain wooden rocking chair, gently rocking back and forth, her head deep in her chest. A kind of snoring sound came from her face and made Minette smile. "That's Baba, my grandmother. She's nearly 90 years old. Actually she's my great-grandmother, but we all call her Baba. That means *Grandmother*."

At that moment, the woman's head came up, as if she knew she was being talked about. She squinted her eyes to adjust to the light and to see the stranger in the kitchen. "Liebchen," she called to Minette as she recognized her granddaughter. Then followed a stream of words that Lili couldn't understand, full of throat-clearing German sounds.

Minette answered the old woman with similar sounds, and turned to Lili. "She doesn't speak English yet. I'm teaching her, but she's hard of hearing and she doesn't really want to learn."

"Gooten morgan, Baba," Lili almost shouted at the woman.

Baba's head turned toward the strange voice. "Gooten after-noon," she returned, nodding her head and smiling as she spoke the English word.

"Yes, I guess it is afternoon. But I don't know how to say that in German."

"Oh, she's not speaking German," Minette corrected. "She's speaking Yiddish. They're alike sometimes, but a little different."

"I like your grandmother," Lili told her friend. "She has a sense of humor; she's not stuffy. My grandmother… my step-grandmother… is very stuffy. The other one always has a twinkle in her eye. Hey, she speaks French." Until that moment Lili hadn't considered her grandmother's French Canadian words unusual. In fact, she had heard her mother chatting with her grandmother in French and she often joined them for a word or two.

"Wouldn't it be wonderful if your grandmother could meet mine?" Lili suggested. "But mine lives so far away."

After a pause, Lili came up with another idea. "Would your grandmother like to meet Anna's grandmother? She speaks German; I'll bet they would understand each other."

Minette's mother hurriedly offered the girls another rugelach and attempted to change the subject. German and Jewish grandmothers had little to say to each other those days. Such a meeting was out of the question.

"Why don't you show Lili your room, Tata. You can take two more pastries with you. And here are two glasses of milk."

"Good idea. Thanks, Mama. Come on, Lili, I'll show you my room."

On the way, Lili noticed a shiny black piano in the living room. "Who plays the piano?" she asked.

"I do, sometimes."

Lili stopped to look at the music standing on the holder and was surprised to see very difficult stuff. "You play this?" she asked, noticing the four sharps that indicated the very difficult key of E. Lili had taken piano lessons before she started playing the violin and she recognized difficult when she saw it. Four sharps was difficult.

"Yes. That's a concert piece I'm working on for the recital."

"Would you play for me? Please?"

Minette sat down, adjusted the music, placed her hands on the keys, took a deep breath and started to play. Ripples of notes tumbled about under her fingers, flew around the room and landed back on the next set. Minette's fingers moved so fast, Lili couldn't keep track of them. She held her breath.

As Minette completed the passage, she stood up matter-of-factly and grabbed back the pastry she had asked Lili to hold. "Come on, I want to show you my room."

Still breathless, Lili whispered, "Minette. You never told me. You're wonderful. You play the piano... like a professional... are you? Professional?"

"I don't know what that means. I've studied for a while."

"How long?"

"Four or five years."

"Ooh, I never knew anyone who could play... really play the piano. And you never said a word."

"To tell the truth, sometimes I'd rather play baseball than the piano. My mother insists I practice when I'd much rather be out playing ball with my brother. Of course, he has to study for Hebrew school, but that's another thing I'm not allowed."

"Because you play the piano?"

"No, because I'm a girl. He gets to do all the neat things — go to Hebrew school, play baseball, help Dad at his business. I get to practice the piano..." Minette accented the words in a girlie voice as she swung her hips. "... and learn to cook."

Lili swallowed the last of her rugelach and grinned broadly. "Not a bad idea if you can learn to make these."

As Lili discovered more about Jewish traditions from her friend Minette, she began to see how much Jews and Christians were alike. She couldn't understand why there might be misunderstandings between them. And she couldn't understand why one group would want to do away with the other.

Anna's mother made strudel that tasted almost the same as Minette's mother's rugelach. The women sounded much the same when they spoke their own languages. Some of them came from the same country, although Minette explained that many of the Jews in her neighborhood came from Russia.

As Lili learned more about tolerance and cultures and people different from her family, she found less and less to understand about the open dissension at her school. Still, she was not ready to introduce her Indian inheritance to her classmates.

The scathing words continued at school, whether shouted by Jew or German. The girls watched, perched on the bars of the metal fence, huddled against the building to escape the chill wind, stalled in mid-game at a hopscotch pad, or walking leisurely across the block-wide asphalt-paved playground.

Lili wrote in her diary how she was sure the words were those they had heard from their parents. She wrote how girls mostly listened and weren't loud and violent like the boys. And girls certainly didn't hate. Hate and fighting were for boys, not for girls. The girls just listened and felt the anger the boys borrowed from their parents and repeated as next-generation's outrage.

She also noted: perhaps the boys are afraid they'll have to go off to war someday themselves.

The War Spreads

*PEARL HARBOR, HAWAII, December 7, 1941 – "A
date that will live in infamy," were the words President
Franklin Delano Roosevelt used to describe the bombing
of Pearl Harbor by the Japanese on that dreadful Sunday
morning.*

LILI'S FEELINGS ABOUT THE WAR were piling up in several
layers of intensity. Deep down she'd come to feel great
sadness for the dirge that was being played around the
world. She hated the war clouds that moved in to hang
over the earth like a gloomy umbrella. On the surface,
she grew tired of repetition, of shortages, of doing
without pleasures she had grown up with.

Food items were disappearing from grocery shelves,
the everyday foods becoming scarce as worldwide
shipping was interrupted. Other items were in short
supply as resources were deflected to fill the military's
growing needs.

Somewhere deep in her soul Lili knew that, like all
seasons, spring would happen, that the war in Europe
would end, that fighting would end, that life would
begin again. But when? All she knew was that she was
being robbed of a precious part of childhood.

Then war came even closer to Milwaukee.

On that Sunday in December 1941, she hadn't yet
experienced the worst effects of war. She had no idea
what the next few years would bring. At one-thirty-five

p.m. (CST) on December 7, 1941, the world became still uglier. Mutters and whispers turned into tormented screams throughout an insane world. Suspicion grew in proportion to the growing fear.

Lili had heard newsboys shouting "Extra, Extra" in radio plays and in movies. But on that cold Sunday afternoon in December she heard the calls of real newsboys as they ran up and down Center Street, even down her own 50th Street, waving their newspapers and calling, "Extra, extra. Read all about it. Pearl Harbor bombed."

Harold Hoffman and his brother had gone to the movies at the Uptown Theater that Sunday. The newsboys were summoned out of the movies by their supervisor from the newspaper, handed stacks of the bold headlines, and sent to cover their routes with the extra edition.

A bomb had fallen into Lili's life. From that moment to the "Extra, Extra" that signaled the ending of the war nearly four years later, she put growing-up on hold and lived an eternity. She came to wish for the end of the war as fervently as she once longed each April for the end of the Wisconsin winter.

Where were you when…? Everyone who lived through those tumultuous times remembers that infamous Sunday, where they were and what they were doing.

Lili and her family had returned from church and were about to sit down to a roast beef dinner when they heard the voices in the street. Boys were calling, "Extra! Extra! Read all about it. Japs Bomb Pearl Harbor, Extra! Extra!"

Lili grabbed a coat and went onto the front porch with her father. "What are they saying, Daddy?"

In a voice she had never heard before, her father whispered, "It's war." When she turned around to look at him, his dusky face had gone pale, reflecting the fresh snow that clung to branches of the fir trees and the shrubbery. The icy sting of his words wound around her tummy and sent an ache throughout her body.

"Let's get a paper," he continued very quietly, waving his hand at the passing newsboy. The boy, a bundle of newspapers under his arm, came up to the porch and handed the paper to Lili as her father dug through his pocket for a dime.

"We're going to war," the boy half shouted. "Thanks, mister," he added, pocketing the dime and turning back down the walkway.

"War, Daddy?" Lili asked as they went back inside. "Are we going to rescue France and England and Greece?"

"Not right now, sweetheart," he answered in a trance as he read the article under the headline: "Pearl Harbor Bombed."

"Where is that?"

"In Hawaii, I think."

"Who's doing the bombing?"

"Japan."

"But we're not fighting the Japanese."

"We're going to war with Japan. They bombed our army base in Hawaii, at Pearl Harbor." He dropped the paper into Lili's hands and walked to the dining room to relate the story to his wife. "We're going to war…" he began.

"I heard," Lili's mother said, spooning gravy over Angel's potatoes. "But not right this minute. Come, eat dinner while it's warm."

"Rosemary, it's war," Lili's dad continued. "We're all in it now — in Europe, in Russia, and now in the Pacific. I've got to…"

Rosemary's head went up and she held the spoon loosely as it dripped gravy on the tablecloth. "No, George, no. You don't have to *anything* right now. Sit down and eat. Lili?" she called, and returned to her own chair, the spoon still dripping.

Lili had read enough about the war to know what was going on. She had two thoughts. "Mom, don't you want Daddy to do his job, his duty?" and then the second thought, "Oh golly, that means he'll have to go away." She said nothing more.

"Are you going to get killed, Daddy?" Angel piped up, her mouth full of potato.

No one spoke for a long time. Lili stood, still holding the newspaper; her father sat down quietly and fingered his napkin; her mother stared at her husband in silence; and Angel went on pushing food into her mouth.

At last, George spoke warmly to his daughter. "No, Angel, Daddy's not going to get killed. But I may have to go away for a bit." Rosemary swallowed a sob, put down the spoon, and slowly left the room.

"Go ahead, girls, eat your dinner. I'll be right back," George said as he followed his wife into the kitchen.

The girls heard their voices but not their words, first softly, then louder, then soft again. When they returned to the table, Lili's mother's face was flushed, and tears stained the cheeks she powdered every Sunday. Lili's father sat down carefully and picked up his fork. "Pass the potatos, please," he said calmly, managing to smile at both his daughters.

George Deveroux appeared at the recruiting station the next day, along with hundreds, maybe thousands, of other young men. He filled out papers and answered questions until they got to the ones about family.

"Married?"

"Yes."

"Children?"

"Yes, two."

"Sorry, Mac, we ain't taking married men with kids today. Let's leave this war to the young single guys. Go home. But thanks for trying."

George didn't tell that story to his family for many years. He simply said his farm-related job kept him out of the army. He could have been called any time the draft got around to men with families. They never got to George Deveroux.

Lili Doesn't Need Ration Stamps For Harold

WASHINGTON DC, February 1942 – The Office of Price Administration has announced a stringent program of rationing to take effect among the American people. Many items have been placed on the list of shortages and will be rationed out using a system of ration stamps.

AS THE UNITED STATES HEADED INTO WAR on two fronts, the Office of Price Administration (OPA) instituted a stringent program of rationing — food, fuel, materials of war that were being earmarked to go overseas to support U.S. troops, "our boys overseas".

Such items included almost everything in Lili's life — sugar, meat, dairy foods, steel, tin, rubber, gasoline, oil, and more. "Everything I want is rationed," Lili moaned.

"It's all going to the war effort, Lili. Don't complain," her mother answered in that maddening way — when mothers speak the truth that daughters don't want to hear.

"But when will it be over?" Lili whined.

"When the boys come marching home. After the duration."

"I heard that Doreen's mother has five bags of sugar in her cupboard. She bought them before rationing started. Why didn't you?"

"That's called hoarding, Lili. It isn't right. We need to share what we have equally… with everyone. If we all hoarded, our boys overseas wouldn't have what they need to fight for us." And that was how each conversation ended. "… for our boys overseas…" and "… for the duration."

Rationing had become an accepted part of life. It also became the reason that the wonderful Harold spent almost an entire wonderful evening with Lili. She could almost forgive the OPA its restrictions. Ah bliss! Here's how it happened.

Periodically, the OPA issued new ration books that contained stamps for householders to use to buy certain commodities that were in short supply. Mostly food and fuel. To do this, public schools were used as distribution points and school children were asked to help out, as ushers, go-fers, telephone answerers, and helpers in a variety of ways. The schools in the 1940s were community centers, places for voting in elections, meeting sites for community purposes, and neighborhood touch points for both social and community events.

Harold and Lili found themselves one such evening in February 1942 on the same work team. She was proud to have been one of the sixth graders chosen to cover the school office, answering phones and relaying messages to the gym where volunteers distributed the ration books. Harold was one of the runners, providing messenger service between the gym and the office. It all worked out rather well.

As the evening wore on, the two sixth graders had run into each other often. Harold started hanging out in the office instead of staying in the gym between messages. To Lili's astonishment, he seemed to be paying more attention to her than he ever had in the past.

Was he dallying near her desk? Was he smiling at her? Why is he the only one coming to the office to check for messages?

After the flurry of the early hours' rush, the phone ceased to ring and people came in smaller numbers, less often. There seemed to be more messengers and helpers than there were things to do.

Harold took advantage of the lull and asked Lili if she would like to walk around the school building. "The school is different at night," he told her. "Aren't you curious?"

All the action of the rationing project was relegated to the basement gym area and Harold continued casually, "I wonder what our floor looks like at night. Want to walk up and take a look?" Lili tried to use an excuse about staying near the phones, maintaining responsibility, but you can imagine it didn't take much coaxing for her to agree.

"Sure," she said, and off they went.

Climbing the familiar terrazzo stairs in the dimness of nightlights seemed strange. Only a few weak bulbs kept the hallways from complete darkness, lending a spooky atmosphere to their daytime image. As they neared the third floor, the pair tiptoed and began to whisper. "This is scary," Lili barely breathed.

"Nah," Harold whispered bravely, "it's just dark."

"It feels scary," she repeated.

As if to calm her fears, or maybe just to guide her, Harold reached over and took her hand, holding it carefully somewhere in the space between them. She felt her breath stop completely as she stared straight ahead into the darkness.

"There's your classroom," Harold pointed out. *So he knows where my room is*, she thought, *even though we're not in the same class. He knows who I am! He knows I'm alive!* Lili's heart began to sing as they walked hand-in-hand through the darkness.

"There's yours," she returned the compliment. Of course she knew where his room was, as well as which seat he occupied. "Do you like Mr. Zarem?" she asked.

"Yeah, he's okay," Harold conceded.

In that moment Lili's world changed, irrevocably, everlastingly, and forever more. It would never be the same again.

Harold let go of her hand and slipped his arm around her shoulders. He held her lightly and pulled her slightly towards him. She thought her heart would pound away the glory of the moment, but it stayed quietly in her body as Lili received her first kiss. The lightness of his lips on her cheek surprised her, and she felt warm and comfortable inside.

Her surprise at the speed with which he maneuvered the kiss didn't come until later when she had a chance to relive the moment. It was then she began to feel what love and friendship are all about. She began to feel the forecast of the woman she was soon to become.

Harold Hoffman and Lili Deveroux never became an item. Their brief infatuation never went any further than that kiss that night in the darkened corridor on the third floor outside Mr. Zarem's classroom at William T. Sherman Elementary School.

Lili never told anyone, not even Megan. She didn't even write it in her diary. She kept it only in her memory.

The GS (Girl Scouts)
SG (Sixth Grade)
and SC (Safety Cadets)

WASHINGTON, DC, March 21, 1942 — Spring officially arrived today, but thousands of young men and women are not at home to see it. Many are following Gen. Douglas MacArthur on his way to Australia where he will organize the American offensive against Japan, including the relief of the Philippine Islands which fell in December. MacArthur, who broke through Japanese lines to leave Corregidor, has promised, "I came through and I shall return."

LILI WAS ELEVEN AND A HALF YEARS OLD the day Pearl Harbor was bombed, in the middle of her sixth year in school. She wrote in her diary that she wasn't quite sure she understood what was happening; what she felt was excitement. Something different was coming into her life — total war.

War was a completely new concept for anyone born after 1918, the end of World War I, "the war to end all wars". For one thing, her life during the first eleven years, six months had been comfortable, warm, and secure. Only in recent months had the shortages begun. Now she realized how curious she was about everything and how objective.

She received a new diary as a Christmas present that year the Pacific war began, and she wrote in it: "I want to know everything and do everything. I want to read every book in the library. I want to learn everything there is to learn."

Still a world at war was something new, something outside herself and her family, something over which she had no control. Before it was over, Lili would write about futility, hate, understanding, conservation, working together, giving up, hope, pain, rationing, glory, bravery, patience, and a thing called *tolerance*.

Milwaukee had a lot of snow that winter. When the family took its holiday trip to northern Wisconsin, her new diary recorded "piles of snow". As long as she could remember, her family had spent Christmas with her mother's sister and New Year's with her father's sister, and with all the grandparents, cousins, aunts, and uncles who could come together for the holidays. Christmas 1941 was not too different from the others.

Lili's diary noted that the weather in January 1942 was a record-breaker, with "the lowest temperatures since 1885, around 25-below all month." That didn't stop her from going to the movies, ice skating, standing at her cadet post at school, taking violin lessons, attending Girl Scout meetings, and attending choir practice, mostly with her friend Megan.

At school, mid-way through the sixth grade, Lili prayed to be moved into Megan's classroom with the teacher that everyone loved. Instead, she drew a second semester with Mrs. Milton, the dour, dreaded teacher who was making Lili's life miserable.

Mrs. Milton was keen on literature, especially poetry, especially Carl Sandburg. Great pictures of the noted poet adorned the walls in her classroom. Lessons included memory sessions to learn his poetry. Lili hated it, but she kept hoping to be switched mid-year. It didn't happen.

"Megan, I don't know if I can stand one more day hearing about the butchering of hogs in Chicago. That woman is obsessed with a poet that does absolutely nothing for me. It's not that I hate him, but I'm leaning that way. She could just push me over the edge."

"Stick with it, Lili," Megan coaxed. "Just remember, we'll all be together in Junior High next year, a long way from her."

"I'll try. Gotta go now, I'm on duty at the corner today."

LILI HAD BEEN A MEMBER of the Sherman School's Safety Patrol since fourth grade. Cadets assisted with street crossings at the school's four corners and served as playground monitors. On playground duty, cadets mostly watched others having fun. But the street corners were another matter.

Sherman School assigned cadets at all four corners around the school each morning, going home and returning at lunchtime, and after school in the afternoon. Usually two cadets were stationed on a corner.

Because the southeast corner, Lili's home corner, was the most heavily trafficked, cadets shared duty with Tony the police officer. Tony handled the motor traffic, and the cadets directed the pupils. (There seemed to be an unwritten rule that children under 12 were *pupils*, and over 12 were *students*.) Lili especially loved directing her sister and her friends.

Sherman School's pupils all went home for lunch. Most of the cadets lived within a couple blocks of the school and had plenty of time to eat a leisurely lunch and get back on duty. Some of the kids lived several blocks and had to rush during the lunch hour, but they managed. Good weather and bad, autumn, winter, and spring.

Cadets met weekly for assignments. As an organization, they trained to perform their duties in an atmosphere that forged and upheld a tight bond of service and dedication. Cadets were issued badges — metal disks about four inches in diameter, painted yellow with black lettering. In the center of each badge was a white safety cross against a black square. These badges were either strapped to the arm or carried by hand; cadets slipped their fingers through the leather strap.

The group elected its officers, lieutenants who carried greater responsibility. Lieutenants were identified by a white strap worn across the chest. Lili was one of the Patrol's dedicated cadets, although she never was elevated to lieutenant.

Oh, the importance of being a cadet! Cadets were allowed to leave class early to take their stations on street corners and to return after the bell when all other pupils were at their desks. Cadets assisted at air raids and fire drills, using their badges to keep the little ones in line and safe. Cadets carried the authority at the street to hold children back or allow them to cross, waving their arms to show who was looking out for them.

Cadets stood a bit taller, held their heads a bit straighter, walked with almost a swagger. They were a proud bunch.

In the late spring of 1942, the Safety Cadets of WTS and other Milwaukee public schools were treated to a weekend at the scenic Wisconsin Dells, traveling by bus on Friday and returning Sunday afternoon. They stayed in a kind of boarding house with large screened porches and big rooms that served as dormitories, the boys in one room, the girls in another. Some even slept on the screened porches. They ate breakfast in a common dining room and had themselves one heck of a time, enjoying freedom from parents, the great beauty of the Dells, and the friendship of others their own age.

Wisconsin Dells then was a sleepy resort town. About twenty cadets from William T. Sherman Elementary joined a hundred or so other Milwaukee cadets for the trip. Lili was there, with her friends Minette and Mary Beth. And Harold also was there. The boys and girls met briefly in breakfast lines, but formed separate groups most of the time, however much Mary Beth and Minette pushed Lili to sit with Harold.

The kids took excursions to the Upper and Lower Dells, enjoyed an evening program in a natural amphitheater, tramped the woods around the town and visited local ice cream shops.

The town in 1942 was only a few blocks long, geared to tourism even then, but quietly so. Townspeople shared their homes with tourists; small shops sold post cards and souvenirs, and restaurants expected crowds in summer. Shade trees lined the streets and a feeling existed similar to a day at the beach or a visit to a Wisconsin lake.

The best part of the entire trip was the re-telling of the adventure when the cadets returned to school, along with the prestige at having spent time away from parents for a few days.

LILI STRUGGLED THROUGH CLASSES with Mrs. Milton. One warm spring day, Lili and Etta had been discussing something important during recess. When they returned to the classroom, they continued as Mrs. Milton assigned a reading session. In moments all heads were bent over textbooks.

"Can you meet me after school?" Etta whispered to Lili without looking up.

"I've got cadet duty," Lili whispered back.

"What?" Etta couldn't hear. She sat two desks away.

"No talking," came a stern warning from the teacher's desk.

Lili shrugged her shoulders at Etta and tried to mouth the words. Etta still failed to catch the message. Lili leaned over then, repeating in a soft whisper, "Can't. I have…"

"Lili Deveroux!" came Mrs. Milton's loud voice.

"Ma'am?" Lili's head shot up and she caught the stern gaze in Mrs. Milton's eyes.

"Lili Deveroux. Stand up please."

Lili had always been the *good girl* in her classes. She never got into trouble with her teachers. The other students gaped at what was going on, their reading forgotten.

"Lili, I have asked you repeatedly to stop talking. You refused to obey. Now you'll have to pay the consequences."

"But Mrs. Milton…" Lili began.

"No excuses. I have you this time."

Lili felt helpless. She persisted, "But Mrs. Milton, I just…"

"Never mind. You'll be punished. When you finish reading this chapter on the exports of China, you are to write a three-page essay on the geography of Asia, including China."

"That's not fair," Lili bristled. "Nobody else…"

"Nobody else was talking. You will write the essay. And you'll have it on my desk tomorrow." The teacher sat down and returned to whatever teachers did. She addressed the rest of the class with only a stare that sent them back to their reading, leaving Lili standing alone.

Tears came to her eyes. She felt her face grow hot, partly with embarrassment, partly with the injustice, and partly with a rising anger. *She's not fair. She can't punish me like that when I didn't do anything wrong.* In a spontaneous movement, Lili grabbed her sweater and ran crying out the door. In the empty hallway, she headed for safety in the girls' room.

After only a moment, she planned a better escape. She'd go home. That would show that old teacher. She'd go home and make her wonder what happened to her student. Maybe she'll get in trouble.

Lili stepped out of the door, back into the empty corridor and ran down the steps and out the door before she could think another thought. She ran all the way home, appearing at the kitchen door flushed, crying, and ready to burst.

"What on earth…" her mother began. "What's happened to you? Why aren't you in school? It's not time for you to be home for lunch yet."

"I'm not going back. You can't make me. That old cow will pay for this. She'll get in trouble for letting me out of her sight."

"What are you talking about?"

Rosemary Deveroux was not an emotional woman. She seldom allowed herself to become embroiled in emotional outbursts, preferring her children go to their rooms and settle their own problems. Today, she sensed Lili's agitation and called out gently, "Come here, sweetheart. Sit down. What's happened?"

Surprised with her mother's concern, Lili quickly assessed the situation. Leaving school without permission must be something worse than she had imagined. Mrs. Milton really could get in trouble. After all, who knows where her student went?

"She… she…" Lili tried to explain through the sobs.

"Who?"

"Mrs. Milton. She… she scolded me… in front of everybody… and I wasn't doing anything wrong."

"And you ran away?" Lili's mother had guessed the rest. "You must have…"

"Yes. I just ran out. Left the old bag standing…"

"That's not any way to talk about your teacher."

"I can't help it. She made me so angry. I didn't know what else to do."

"And you ran all the way home." Her mother held the child and waited until the sobs slowed down. "Well now, what will you do next?"

"I don't know." The sudden idea that there would be a *next* stunned Lili. She hadn't thought things through that far. When you're acting out, you don't think ahead.

"Tell you what. Let's have lunch. Angel will be here in a few minutes. You can help me get things ready. Then, after lunch, you wash your face and go back to class, just like nothing happened."

"Oh muh-ther, I couldn't."

"I think you can. Think about it. There isn't much of a choice. The law says you have to be in school unless you're sick. And even if you said you were sick, you'd have to go back sometime. Best it be right away. Get it over with."

Lili wasn't quite ready to admit defeat. "But she said I had to write an essay… as punishment."

"Then write the essay and make it the best one you ever wrote. She'll see who is responsible and who isn't. Any girl who can take her medicine and face up to the consequences will win her respect. I just have a feeling."

Mothers usually aren't that tuned into daughters and what makes them tick. But in this instance, Rosemary Deveroux grabbed a serious problem and turned it into a victory for Lili.

After lunch, Lili returned to school with Angel, walked casually into her classroom without looking at Mrs. Milton, sat down, and began to outline her essay.

The work she turned in the following day was spread across five pages and was a very insightful summary of the geography of Asia, including not only China, but Mongolia, Japan, and Siam, and including the problems of invasion that Japan had instigated in its attempt to conquer the continent. Mrs. Milton never bothered her again.

PATRIOTISM BECAME THE HEARTENING THEME at William T. Sherman Elementary School as the war wore on. That spring all the sixth grade classes learned the same set of songs during music class, the songs representing each branch of the armed services: "The Caisson Song", "Anchors Aweigh", "The Marine Hymn", and the Air Force Song about the "Wild Blue Yonder". The classes took turns practicing the songs while lined up on stage in the school auditorium.

On program day, classes solemnly entered the assembly, quietly walking in lines to their assigned seats: first and second graders up front, third and fourth graders in the middle, and fifth and sixth graders at the back. One by one, the classes trooped to the stage, walked up the steps on either side, took their positions and sang their songs. Lili felt shivers up her spine at the stirring climax of the program as the sixth graders sang out their hearts and lungs honoring the servicemen who were fighting in a war that scattered them all around the world.

Lili and the school orchestra did their bit for the war effort by practicing patriotic songs to present at their now-and-then concerts. Weekly orchestra practice was always more fun than work, with the boys in the trumpet section kidding the girls in the violin section. Lili practiced hard to become a first violinist so she could carry the tune once in a while. Even though the second violinists played much of the background, Lili always claimed the firsts had more fun.

Other wartime assemblies were offered WTS pupils. A variety of speakers made the rounds of schools, relating stories of their own wartime experiences. Lili particularly enjoyed hearing an Italian tenor who sang songs of his native country, ending with a gigantic rendition of "God Bless America". She was intrigued by the Greek and Polish freedom fighters who came to tell their stories of harrowing escapes, daring deeds, all of which ended with a plea for U.S. support.

Closer to home, the principal, Mr. Ulrich — Louis E. Ulrich — led a sad assembly to announce the departure of the physical education teacher who had been called to serve in the Army. Pupils greeted the announcement with mixed emotions, sad at the departure of their friend and not-so-sad that they might have to sacrifice the dreaded P.E. "for the duration".

Before the P.E. teacher left, he rehearsed pupils to participate in a city-wide performance of a routine using crepe paper streamers, drill, and discipline. The children learned a routine of twists and twirls with the streamers and practiced them on the playground to a recorded song. For the performance, pupils all wore white blouses and shirts with dark skirts or pants. They stood at fingertip distance in lines that spread over the whole playground — a city block full of children repeating moves in sequence that were learned in class units. A true William T. Sherman School Spectacular! (Years later, Lili heard the song and could see the colorful paper streamers twirling in unison. She even recalled some of the routine.)

The next question to bother pupils at Sherman School was how many other of the school's men teachers would be called to duty. Certainly Mr. Ulrich was safe; he had white hair and grandchildren. Men with families, older men and those with certain war occupations were exempted from the draft, although many of them enlisted voluntarily. But what about Mr. Kolmas and Mr. Zarem? War indeed was striking closer and closer to home.

Meatless Tuesdays and Other Inconveniences

CASABLANCA, Morocco, October 15, 1942 — From ETO headquarters, Gen. Eisenhower has announced that Gen. Montgomery has routed Field Marshal Rommel and his troops after the Battle of El Alamein. Gen. Eisenhower's goals now shift to planning the invasion of Italy. Troops from the U.S. and Britain are joining forces with the Free French army to re-take Europe.

AFTER THE BOMBING OF PEARL HARBOR, the world shifted into *uglier* as the U.S. became fully geared up for war. Rationing was in full bloom. During that very cold winter, the United States had officially changed to Standard War Time on February 9, 1942.

In March Lili ran for vice president of School Cadets and lost, and ran for orchestra secretary and won. Her sister Angel got her first clarinet and started taking lessons on Saturdays at 8th Street and Walnut.

As big sister, Lili accompanied Angel each Saturday on the trolley. Lili spent the hour that Angel tooted watching men in store windows roll Cuban cigars, smelling the delicious aroma of tobacco as it wafted the street.

It was on Walnut Street that Lili and Angel saw a black person for the first time. Or had one of the ragmen been darker than the others? They weren't sure. The white people on Walnut Street called them Negros. Lili heard their melodic voices and accented words and couldn't wait to get home to tell her mother.

"They're beautiful, Mom," she called as the girls came into the kitchen.

"Who's beautiful?"

"Negros. We saw some today. Down on Walnut Street, where Angel takes her lesson. There were three on the street. They said, 'Good morning'," Lili explained, trying to get the accent just right.

"And they smiled at us," Angel added. "But their skin isn't really black. It's just sorta dark brown, like when Daddy stays in the sun too long in the summer. He gets so dark. Well, they're dark too."

"That may explain why they were called *darkies* in the movies," said Rosemary Deveroux. "I remember hearing that word in a movie I saw many years ago." Their mother looked off into the distance. It had been such a long time since she had gone to a movie.

Lili read in the newspaper once about a platoon of Negro soldiers who had become heros. Then she read about another platoon — American Indian soldiers who were serving their country just as heroically. She felt proud. Lili read the newspaper every day now. As a sixth grader, she wanted to know what was going on in the world.

It seemed to this child, not yet twelve years old, that her country had interests in events all around the world. "Is that why they're calling this a World War?" she asked her father one evening.

"This is the second World War we've had. When I was about your age, we had another one. Supposed to be the war to end all wars."

"Guess it didn't, did it?"

Lili got used to seeing pictures of GIs slogging through jungles, GIs marooned in sandy deserts, GIs perched on top of tanks eating out of small tin cans — and always with big smiles on their faces. Lili couldn't understand what they had to smile about so far from home, being shot at in bug-infested sweaty countries.

Each time she picked up a newspaper, she wondered what it would look like without war news? What did reporters write about before the war? What will they write about after... when... *after the duration*?

One night, Lili woke from a dream believing she had heard shots fired at her. She had dreamed she was carrying a rifle over her shoulder as she went to find a bush to hide under. But she couldn't get it off her shoulder to fire it. Soldiers were shooting at her, yelling something about her uniform being on backward, and she was helpless to defend herself. She tried to yell back at them to stop shooting, but her voice wouldn't work either.

When she woke, she sat up in bed, the damp sheets tangled around her arms. She cried out, then just cried as she wondered if those poor boys overseas felt as helpless when the shooting started as she did sitting there in her bed.

Once the war against Japan had become front-page news, the children at William T. Sherman Elementary School took another look at the world-wide scope of their country's involvement. Strangely, they viewed each other with less animosity, determined to pull together to do what they could for "the war effort". Now the suspicions were aimed outward, directed at *them*, "the enemy". Their school had no Asian students.

Students collected $60 for Infantile Paralysis (later to be called the March of Dimes) and they collected for the war effort. Lili's Girl Scout troop knit for the Red Cross. Celebrations and auditorium programs supported the war effort and showed children how to survive. Maybe the world's parents were the targets of the war, but the kids had to learn the survival techniques.

They learned to hang blankets or heavy curtains at the windows so that light wouldn't escape into the night air to signal the way for some bomber to drop its load on Milwaukee. Although the possibility was remote, it also seemed reasonable because of the location of Milwaukee's Billy Mitchell Air Force Base.

Block air raid wardens came to school to show children where the air raid shelters were located in the school basement and to drill them in getting to the shelters calmly. Large signs lettered "Air Raid Shelter" were hung along the doorways, with arrows pointing down. The children of Sherman School, all under the age of 12, learned to recognize the sounds of air raid sirens and learned to retreat to the basement in orderly rows.

THE FOOD SHORTAGE HIT EVERYONE. Milwaukee had just learned to make hamburgers when the war's meat shortages curtailed the fad. If Lili's family had a roast, it was either pork or a very small cut of beef. Pork was cheap and more abundant; beef went into cans for soldiers. Chicken was more common for everyone. Oddly enough, neither turkey nor mutton was ever rationed.

Then there were the awful meatless dishes — made with noodles, cheese, rice, but no meat. Lili's father, an agriculturist, talked about testing a new product as food, something called *soybeans*. He said it was easy to grow, tasted just like meat and made a very good meatloaf. Lili's mom made some, but nobody ate much. Another of Lili's dad's experiments involved using molasses instead of sugar. Yech! was the resonant criticism.

While rationing brought about creativity in the kitchen, some housewives depended on their charm to solve their culinary problems. They made friends with their butchers; the more adept at flirting received the prized quality cuts.

Meatless Tuesday became a weekly event, the brainchild of some government agency that thought the nation could be convinced to conserve meat by eliminating it from menus one day a week. Before the war was over, the idea would expand to include Wednesdays and Thursdays. Because of the scarcity of ration stamps at the Deveroux house, meat soon came to be served only on Sundays, with substitutes such as Spam, bologna, fish, or cheese on other days.

Critical shortages of other resources were part of the war effort. Metal had gone into the manufacture of tanks and guns; gasoline supplies were drained off to fuel the tanks.

Movies often eased the daily life of war, offering relief from fear and shortages. Movies lent a perspective to the war by presenting accounts of what was going on at the front. Movies solicited support for the war through propaganda. Of course, Lili and Megan didn't know about propaganda; they just enjoyed the movies, usually at the Uptown Theater. Admission to the movies was raised to twelve cents for children under age twelve, to allow for a federal two-cent tax. That modest price included cartoons and war news footage that were shown between double features, with a weekly serial episode thrown in!

One cartoon that tickled their funny bones was a government propaganda film that sought to convince the public to deal with shortages by enjoying Meatless Tuesdays. The cartoon showed a flea that mapped out the host dog's tasty parts like the scoring of beef cattle. Along with the rest of the free world, the flea tired of observing Meatless Tuesdays. It hopped about the dog's body singing a ditty that threw the girls into fits of laughter. This time Lili learned the words first and taught Megan.

Paraphrasing "She'll Be Coming Around the Mountain," the words were: *There's food around the corner, food around the corner, food around the corner for me, Hallelujah Brother....* The second verse was: *There'll be no more meatless Tuesdays, no more meatless Tuesdays, no more meatless Tuesdays for me. Hallelujah Brother....* For some reason this really cracked them up, even more so than other silly tunes: "Three Itty Fishes" and "Maresy Doats."

Sugar was another rationed item. Lili's mother planned and saved for weeks to provide birthday cakes for her family. She tried all sorts of substitutes — the yucky molasses, maple syrup, sugar cane, beet sugar, and sorghum. Sugar substitutes weren't much more popular than the meat substitutes. Lili got used to eating cereal with fruit. In summer, strawberries, raspberries, blueberries, and peaches made wonderful sweeteners.

But berries couldn't sweeten pies and cakes. And berries weren't chocolate, another scarce item. Ice cream and bakery pastries became rare. Bakeries had to ration meager supplies of sugar along with their customers. Lili wondered how they managed to stay in business. Imagine life without proper birthday cakes!

Spring 1942 found Europe in the dark, fallen to the hideous scourge of Nazi tyranny, even as the gentle people of the Pacific fought the terror of invasion and destruction by Japanese armies.

For Lili, spring 1942 was full of violin lessons, rationing, roller skating, movies, air raid drills, Girl Scouts, orchestra, propaganda and Safety Cadets.

Little Girls Can't
Go To War

THE WAR, Summer 1942 – The Russians have turned the tide at Stalingrad.

General Montgomery has saved Egypt; allied forces land in Africa and the Mediterranean.

U.S. troops landed on Midway Island and have begun an offensive there. The feeling in the air is that "we're in a position now to demand unconditional surrender."

THE SGC (SECRET GIRLS CLUB), which initially had begun somewhere in the fourth grade, was still strong going into the sixth grade. By that time, Lili, Megan, Etta, Minette, Doreen, Mary Beth, and Anna had called themselves, at one time or another, the Fateful Five, the Fearless Five, and the Fancy Five. After Mary Beth was added in the fall of 1942, they became the Silly Six, and after Anna joined, the SGC became the Sassy Seven.

They met at the drop of a suggestion on the playground during recess, in each others homes after school, at the park, or on street corners. They still paired off in varying ways: Minette and Etta, Doreen and Mary Beth, Megan and Lili, Anna and Lili, Minette and Megan, Etta and Lili, but the seven carried a bond among themselves that kept them close.

That winter when the United States entered the war in the Pacific, the Fearless Five sat huddled in a corner of the playground talking quietly about what was happening. "My dad is going to Georgia to teach soldiers to use war motorcycles," Megan had announced.

"My dad's already enlisted," Minette whispered. "I sure hope nothing happens to him. He never even liked looking at guns. Now he might have to carry one. Do you suppose?"

"Maybe. There are lots of jobs in the army," Etta offered.

"My dad said he wouldn't have to go because of all of us kids; he wouldn't be drafted, but he wouldn't wait," Minette went on. "Papa says he wants to get to Europe and fight Germans. He says he owes that to our new country, America."

"My dad wants to go so he can invade Holland and save our relatives," Doreen told her friends.

"Do you have relatives in Holland?"

"Oh sure. My grandmother lives there and I have aunts and uncles and cousins. We haven't heard anything from them since the Germans took over."

"How about your dad, Etta?"

At the question, Etta's eyes clouded over and she began to cry. "He's... he's... he may have to go if the draft calls him. They're going to call men with children after the single men," she sobbed. "And that's all he has, my brother and me."

"Don't cry, Etta. Maybe the war will end before they have to call men with children." Lili spoke confidently, but she was just as scared as Etta. Lili's dad wouldn't have to answer the draft until they began to take farmers, she had told her friends. "His job puts him in a classification that's safe — at least for the time being."

How could Lili have guessed how badly her father had wanted to join the action?

"Megan, I saw your dad the other day in Perlman's Grocery and he was wearing a uniform. Is he in the Army?" Anna said.

"No, but he wears the uniform sometimes. He has to wear it when he goes to army camps. Isn't that neat? We all tease him by whistling and calling 'hubba-hubba' when he puts it on."

"He looks just like General Eisenhower," Anna added. "I like General Eisenhower. He's going to show those Nazis where to go."

"Just so Hitler stays out of England," Etta sneered. "I hate the Germans. They're dropping bombs on England, and my mom is afraid they'll invade. What if they do?"

Anna stood up and walked over to the jungle gym.

The other girls sat still until Minette, the Jewish Minette, stood up and followed her. She put her arm around German Anna's shoulders, saying nothing. She didn't have to.

The ideas floated around, fueled by rumors and speculation. England was too much like the United States. If the Nazis took England, would they keep on coming to America? And now the Japanese threatened their country from the other side.

The tiny voice of Etta squeaked out her answer. "They won't dare invade America. Not if my dad is over there." The girls all hugged her as if she and her dad had just saved the world from the treacherous enemy. This war was beginning to touch all their lives.

Those little girls were feeling the two faces of war: glory versus brutality. First there was the romantic side

— a man in uniform has a certain panache that he lacks in street clothes. The idea that their relatives would be roaming the world, looking for adventure, seeing sights they'd never see at home, was exciting to the girls.

But the flip side was the terror, the fear of facing an enemy who hated you enough to shoot at you.

Lili often lay awake at night, waiting, listening for the sound of airplanes to invade the skies over Milwaukee, wondering how she would respond to being forced to enter the army and learn to fire a gun — if she were a boy. She'd listen to Angel's sleep breathing and whisper her fears aloud, "If I were a boy, would I ever point a gun at *them* and fire it? Would I feel anything if I had to throw a hand grenade at *them*." The *them* was nefarious, blurry, not the vision of real people. To Lili, *them* was something she never got around to defining. She couldn't make herself peer into the darkness to see… a person.

Her thoughts routinely envisioned joining the army — if she were a boy. Could she put on a uniform, learn to march and salute, learn to use a gun and clean it? She'd imagined the long train ride to the point of embarkation, the long boat trip to the enemy's country, and then the jeep ride to the front lines. Always the same, she felt the warmth of her friends around her; she couldn't have imagined the loneliness of being away from home. She had never felt hungry or cold; she couldn't imagine crouching in the dark waiting for the light of day to begin firing a gun.

But then, her visions were limited to what she knew about war. And what little girls in Milwaukee in 1942 knew about war was what they had seen in movies — the glory of marching to brave songs, soldiers accompanied by pretty women being fed by caring hands at departing train stations, facing the moment of truth alone, and returning, only slightly wounded, to a hero's welcome.

Either that or the humor of Abbott and Costello, Red Skelton, Ed Wynn, Martha Ray, Betty Hutton and other comedians, who tried to put a lighter face on war. The warriors they portrayed never had to fight or face the demons of war. They just sang and joked their way through it.

War or No War, Girls Grow Up

BURMA, May 1942 — The Japanese have taken over the Burma Road, China's lifeline over the Himalaya mountains. Gen. Chennault's Flying Tigers are keeping the skies above South China clear of Japanese planes as they fly in supplies over "the hump".

As SPRING OF 1942 BROKE INTO BLOSSOM, the SGC renamed itself the Silly Six as it welcomed Mary Beth Kobena to the group. Beth was a musician who usually went straight home from school to practice her violin. She studied seriously with a violinist who had fled Vienna and who took only highly talented students. Her classmates knew that Beth was talented since she sat in first chair in the school orchestra and played solos at concerts.

Still, Mary Beth hadn't been invited to join the SGC until the day Megan and Lili found her crying in the girls restroom. Megan and Lili had gone to wash paint brushes and Beth had slipped out of orchestra.

"It's nothing," Beth insisted. "I'm just being silly."

"What is it, Beth?" Lili asked. "Something is making you cry, silly or not."

"Silly sounds like us," Megan quipped.

"I don't know. I'm, you know, I'm starting to… become a… a… woman. My mother says."

"You mean, you…" Beth nodded.

"But aren't you our age? Twelve?"

Beth nodded again. "Yes, I turned twelve just before Christmas."

"Oh wow," Megan's eyes widened. "All that stuff Mother gave me to read? It actually happens? When you're twelve?"

"What things?" Lili was in the dark. Her twelfth birthday was still weeks away.

"You know, girl things," Megan tried to help her friend understand, but she felt awkward talking about it. "Tell you what, I'll show you The Booklet my mother gave me, next time you come over. Maybe it's time we all read it. I just didn't think it would start this soon."

"What would start?" Lili was beginning to feel left out of the conversation.

"Hasn't your mother talked to you yet? Or given you The Booklet?"

"What booklet?"

"The Booklet," Beth and Megan chimed in. Beth had forgotten her tears and was trying to help out.

"Let's call a meeting of the SGC club, make Beth a new member and bring The Booklet for…" Megan left out Lili's name, finishing graciously, "…everyone to read."

"Let's meet at my house," Beth offered. "My folks will be at work and we won't be disturbed."

"Oh, that's right, your mother is a doctor too, just like your dad," Megan remarked. "Let's meet Friday after school, and I'll tell the others."

"And thanks for making me feel better. I thought I was such a moron for feeling this weird." Beth had dabbed cold water on her eyes and was ready to get back to orchestra practice.

"Know what the little moron said about his new spring suit?" Lili was trying to cheer them up as well as change the subject.

"Yeah," Megan moaned, "Now I don't have to worry about falling down."

"Oh, you've heard it," Lili answered. "I gotta go now."

Friday after school the six girls started toward Beth's house. She lived across from the Catholic Church, a place that held the mysteries of the ages for the girls. None of them even knew a Catholic. The neighborhood Catholic children all attended school at the church — a parochial school — another new phrase for Lili to learn.

"Let's go inside," Megan exclaimed suddenly as they approached the corner.

"No, we couldn't," the others shrieked.

"Why not? Nothing will happen."

The girls tried to keep walking, but Megan held back. "Come on, scaredy cats. Come on, I'll go first. Call my mom if I disappear." Megan turned into the sidewalk that ran beside the rose garden and led to a side door. Lili tried to catch her arm, but Megan was off. Lili followed, with Minette and Etta behind.

"I can't," Beth tried to squirm away. "My parents don't allow me in this church."

"That does it. Neither does mine," Doreen said, adding, "We're Dutch Reformed. I think we don't like Catholics."

"My parents are Greek Orthodox," Beth said evenly, as if that explained her parents' warning.

"Well mine like to explore churches," Megan said breezily, grabbing Lili's hand and continuing towards the door. "Come on. I promise it won't hurt." As soon as she had said the words, she began to wonder if she could make good her promise.

"Hey, don't leave us here!" Doreen and Beth ran to catch up with their friends.

The girls formed a tight shivering pack and proceeded toward the door, their bodies bent slightly to appear smaller. "I wish I were invisible," Minette whispered.

"We are, didn't you know?" Megan shot back over her shoulder. "Grownups hardly ever notice children."

Just as the girls reached the door, it opened and a large nun dressed in full black habit walked past them. "Good afternoon, girls," she said, smiling at them and moving off down the path past the roses.

"See?" Though Megan's heart was pounding almost out of her body, she took a deep breath and beamed at her friends. "See? Nuns are nice."

Megan caught the door before it swung shut and ushered the girls inside. They stood in a tight circle as their eyes adjusted to the dim lighting.

"I can't see," Doreen whined.

"I shouldn't be here," Beth added.

"I have to go to the bathroom," Minette said.

"Shhhh," said Megan.

In a few moments, the hallway in front of them began to take shape as their eyes began to focus. The girls saw the pictures on the wall, the booklets and papers that lay on small tables, and plants, lots of green lacy potted plants along the walls and in the corners. And not one sign of fire and brimstone, Lili thought, but she said nothing.

"This way," Megan beckoned down the hall. The girls stuck close together and followed. At a closed door, they jumped up and down trying to peek through a window that was set too high for them to see.

"I think it's a chapel," Megan whispered as she put her hand on the door panel and pushed, just a bit.

The door opened, and the girls caught a whiff of something unusual but enticing — incense. They saw the nuns before they heard them begin to sing. The music sounded familiar, churchy, and the girls stood still, listening.

A soft voice behind them asked, "Beautiful, isn't it? Did you want something?" The girls turned as one and came face to face with an angel, a nun with a face that appeared full and pink and heavenly. "Can I help you?" she asked.

"We, we, we..." Doreen stuttered. "We... we were looking for... for..." Lili tried to continue for her friend. "We're looking for the restroom," Minette brought the sentence to an end.

"Ah, I see. You're not students here, are you?" she said, looking directly at each girl. When she saw the girls look at each other, she didn't wait for an answer, but continued, "Right over there. Please be very quiet. We're having prayers."

The girls, relieved at her kindness, stood basking in the glow of her angelic eyes, not moving. The nun continued, "We're teachers. It's the end of the day. We pray for our students… and ourselves," she smiled again.

"Come on," whispered Minette. "I've gotta go." The girls half backed their way down the hall, still enchanted by the nun with the angelic face.

"Thank you, Sister," Megan said politely. She had regained her poise and remembered to call the nun *Sister*.

The girls crowded into the small restroom, and suddenly they all had to use it. Minette first, then the others, taking turns. At last, they smoothed their skirts, checked the mirror, patted their hair, and picked up their jackets. Their heads held high, they walked in single file down the hallway, back to the door, and out into the late afternoon sunlight.

Once outside, they ran, as fast as they could straight to Beth's house where they fell into the kitchen and rolled on the floor, laughing their relief and confusion. They had forgotten the purpose of their visit to Beth's and spent the remainder of their time together talking about the nun with the angelic face and wondering what it took to become a Catholic.

The next week Beth brought The Booklet to school, and during recess the SGC met to read it.

"Look at the drawing," said Etta, pointing to the diagram of a female reproductive system. "What does that mean?"

Nobody could explain the connection between that and what Beth had told them happened to her. "There was blood…"

"Oooh yucky," Minette turned away, not interested.

"…and I had to wear a pad to catch it. It wouldn't stop, not for a couple days."

"Didn't you feel weak?"

"Well, sort of funny, but not weak. There wasn't that much blood. And it wasn't all the time. It kind of came and went."

"I think I'll stay in bed when it happens to me," said Lili. "I just couldn't walk around when that was going on."

"Actually, I kind of forgot about it after the first day," said Beth.

The girls read pieces of the literature, each of them curious about one aspect or another, but all of them failing to accurately figure out just what was supposed to happen — and why.

"To think that this goes on until we're old ladies," Beth, daughter of two doctors, finally offered.

"Really?" Minette wondered vaguely.

"Yup, every month until we're old," Beth repeated. "Something to look forward to, huh?"

Again the girls fell silent. None of them could imagine how long that would be.

VERY SOON SCHOOL WAS OVER FOR THE SUMMER and the SGC disbanded until September. When they'd meet again, the girls would be in junior high school.

Once, in late July, Doreen's family invited the girls to join them at their cottage at the lake. The outing counted as a Girl Scout outing, since Doreen's mother often helped her daughter's troop leader. At the lake, Doreen's father taught the girls about boats and sailing and swimming.

Lili packed a large suitcase with play clothes. Her mother referred to her children's clothes as *school, church, dress up*, and *play*. Each outfit was appropriate for certain times and events, others were not. The play clothes often were worn-out school clothes.

This summer, Lili's mother had made her a pair of dark green slacks and a pair of brown shorts. Pants for girls were something very new then, and Lili felt very fashionable. She also packed her swimsuit, a notebook to keep a record of the experience, and several blouses that had seen better days in the schoolroom.

"If this is a cottage, I'll be a monkey's uncle", Lili wrote in her journal the first night. *"It looks like a real house, with a porch, living and dining room, kitchen, and bedrooms. We all sleep in a room on the second floor. There are several cots and we share the indoor bathroom downstairs. It's fun!!!!"*

The three days flew by as the girls learned how to sail, kayak, and save each other from drowning — all to earn their Girl Scout water safety badge. They walked down the road each day to the mailbox and walked into the small town one evening for ice cream. And they giggled a lot. Never had Lili enjoyed herself without her family as she did during that weekend with her Girl Scout friends.

The best part, they all agreed, was the talking in the dark after lights-out when they shared their deepest thoughts and ideas. That's when Lili admitted she wanted to become a journalist, maybe even a newspaper reporter.

BECAUSE OF THE GASOLINE SHORTAGE, most families didn't travel much during the war years. Lili's family was luckier than most because her dad had a farm-related job and therefore was issued an A-card. That meant he traveled in a critical line of work, which entitled him to more gasoline. It wasn't enough to make travel much of an option, but the car didn't have to sit in the garage as many other cars did. For the first time, Lili's family spent both the Fourth of July and Christmas by themselves, not traveling north to visit relatives.

Megan's father, working for the motorcycle plant, had taken to driving a Harley-Davidson back and forth to work. That spring he sold the family car.

Horses, that were being retired at the onset of the war, were brought back into service to haul milk and pull other delivery trucks as well as garbage wagons. The dairy serving the Deveroux family continued house-to-house deliveries with those wonderful old horse-drawn wagons. The horses quickly learned the routes and seemed to know just how far to go and when to stop for each delivery. Lili loved to hear the clip-clop of the horses' hooves as they came down the alley, accompanied by the gentle clinking of milk bottles.

In time, Lili didn't think about rationing often. It just *was*. Nearly everyone adjusted to it "for the duration of the war". When she longed for something — a bike, ice skates, a new dress, a sweater, a new refrigerator for the family — she learned to censor the wish quickly. She knew there was no steel or rubber for bicycles, ice skates, cars, and refrigerators, and she knew that wool and cotton fabrics were earmarked for military uniforms. She also knew that sugar, vanilla, chocolate, rubber, coconut, tea, and spices came from countries that were occupied by enemy troops.

Hoarding equaled a treachery that patriotic Americans found abominable. *Hoard* became a dirty word and those who stockpiled scarce commodities were scorned. "Support the war effort" were the by-words that kept Americans going.

Still, there were people who trafficked in black market items, stockpiled their larders and snubbed their noses at shortages, claiming they knew the government had "plenty of everything". These people became the villains to the kids. However, like the UFOs of the future, everybody talked about them, but nobody had actually seen one.

Radio, Newspapers, Films

Summer 1942: War at its worst. Germans increase air power with their new jet Messerschmitts as U-boats withdraw from U.S. coast. Jews are led to death camps. Japanese make gains in Pacific and take over Guadalcanal.

THE MIGHTY WAR OF THE MEDIA was almost as loud as the war going on around the world. All of them played and re-played the message: "support American troops, the boys overseas". Not only did Bob Hope begin his annual USO Christmas trips to service units overseas, but the movie business at home took on a different character.

The growing film era of the 1930s had reached its heights with color films — "Gone With the Wind", "Bluebird of Happiness", and "Wizard of Oz" — before the war. Now came films about courageous freedom fighters of France, Norway, the Balkans, Greece, Italy, and Great Britain. Movies were about mysterious North Africa, the desert, and the intrigue of spies everywhere.

Outright military battles were depicted realistically on-screen in the mud of Italy, the sands of exotic Pacific Islands, in the dense jungles of the South Pacific, anywhere in the air, on or under the seas, and in far-off lands where America's "boys" were fighting. All were filmed on studio lots in California. Some of the films were outright pitches for men and women to sign up for military service.

Recruiting films abounded and recruiting offices turned up near movie theaters. Janet Leigh and Bette Davis showed how servicemen had good times in USOs and Stagedoor Canteens. The casts of those movies read like "Who's Who in Hollywood". Star after star trooped merrily across the stage to add their names — big names and lesser-known names — to the show bill. Hollywood was doing its bit to support the war effort. The message was clear: "join the military service and make your country proud."

A few films tried humor to keep the American public going — movies with Katharine Hepburn and Claudette Colbert slugging it out with Spencer Tracy and Clark Gable in the war of the sexes, Bud Abbott and Lou Costello winning battles against the army as well as the nation's enemies, Bob Hope and Bing Crosby traveling exotic "Roads" to bring laughter to war-weary audiences. Even a few musicals were added to the screen to provide pure let's-sit-back-and-forget-the-war entertainment.

Newspapers became Lili's greatest passion, becoming both solace and enigma. She read them every day, following battles through maps and stories, learning of heroic actions, reading stories of bravery and courage as well as stories of casualties and lost beachheads. Would the war ever end? What would journalists write about if there were no casualty lists, stories of progress in this Pacific Island battle or on that Italian hillside? Months seemed like years to 12-year-old Lili. Years became lifetimes.

Constant messages flew over the radio airwaves — buy bonds, save scrap metal, keep up the morale of servicemen overseas. Late at night when Lili was babysitting, she'd scan the short-wave radio dial, listening for messages from war zones. More often she found Mexican music from Del Rio, Texas.

"Don't talk about war secrets, Loose Lips Sink Ships." Children greatly feared even hearing anything that sounded like war news that might benefit the enemy. Who knew who *They* were, where *They* lurked, how *They* were listening?

Pupils of William T. Sherman Elementary School learned to re-use and recycle, although those weren't the terms used then. They saved cooking fat that could be strained to make soap. People brought cooking grease to stores where they were reimbursed by storekeepers who then sold it for re-use by the military.

The kids collected metal, especially iron, steel, and aluminum. They collected rubber, string, paper, cloth fabric, just about everything. Sherman School held Scrap Rubber Days when kids hauled to school all the rubber things they had scavenged. Some boys even dragged old tires along, treasures they had found by scouring empty lots. No one was ever sure why, but the kids saved the tinfoil used as liners in gum wrappers and other foodstuffs. The foil had to be scraped away from the paper, then formed into balls that grew larger — like snowballs — with each day of saving.

The children saved paper. They bundled newspapers and carried them to pick-up areas. At school no piece of writing paper went into the wastebasket until it had been used on both sides. Wartime children for years found it difficult to discard a piece of paper that hadn't been completely used.

Recycling, called *conservation* for the war effort, was not only politically correct, it was a way of life. Housewives pulled their children's wagon to the store to carry food in paper bags that were used and re-used. Newspaper was used to wrap carrots and celery while used bags were okay for potatoes and onions. Even burlap bags and wooden bushel baskets were saved and re-sold.

CHILDREN SAVED MONEY IN SPECIAL WAYS. They earned an auspicious sum of a penny-a-pound by saving scrap materials and brought their change to school on Wednesdays to buy Defense Stamps.

Lili stashed away her babysitting money, part of her allowance, and any change she could get her hands on to bring to school on Wednesdays. Sometimes it was only a dime. Other days she would bring as much as four dimes. She would proudly walk to the front of the class, in turn, and plunk down her money to buy the stamps.

She secured the stamps in a special hiding place, usually a pocket in her dress, or the corner of her handkerchief, and rushed home after school to paste them in her stamp book. Slowly, slowly, the book began to fill. When a book was full, it was worth $18.75, which bought a war bond (E-Series) that matured to $25 in ten years.

The competition was wild. When someone did bring enough to buy a whole bond outright (or heavens! two), the class cheered and thanked the buyer.

Lili wrote in her diary, *Miss Schlueter's class collected $12.40 cents in stamps today. And one person bought a bond, the entire thing with $18.75! Must be some rich kids in there.*

"That's all right," called Lili's collection monitor. "We collected $8.70 in stamps. And Nell has promised her dad will give her money for a bond next week. We'll beat them next week for sure." While occasionally some rich kid's parents sent them to school with $75 to buy a $100 bond, most of the children were *turtles* — those who conscientiously saved pennies, nickels, and dimes and brought in small amounts each week.

This was part of life at William T. Sherman Elementary School that continued as normally as possible under wartime conditions. Lili bought her first war bond with her stamp collection on May 20, 1942.

Lili had reached her twelfth birthday that summer and celebrated without a birthday cake. She received another Louisa May Alcott book and a set of watercolors and brushes, but not the bicycle she had hoped for.

According to her diary, she paid the first full price at the movies — twenty-five cents. (She paid the increased price then, but managed to get by as a "child" until Thanksgiving.)

BY SUMMER 1942, LILI AND MEGAN had built their doll collection to eighteen. Just when they thought they had run out of countries, they discovered another one. Morocco. As the battles of North Africa filled the newspapers and brought new countries into prominence, the girls wondered about the people in that country. Their Moroccan doll became a favorite because they had a good time finding pictures of Moroccan people. Megan called this her best work, and Lili felt it looked a bit like herself.

Their doll collection started to draw attention from both parents and teachers. In the fall, their geography teacher, Miss Norton (at Steuben Junior High), called the newspapers, and the girls were interviewed and photographed for a newspaper article. The item was accompanied with a picture of the girls holding their latest dolls.

"We're famous!" cried Megan when she saw herself on page three of the People Section.

"Gosh," was all Lili could manage. At last she had found her name and her picture in the newspapers.

"You can be proud of yourselves," Lili's mother said, hugging both girls together. "Your dad and I are proud of you." She squeezed Lili's shoulder. "Both of you," she added as she wiped a lock of hair off Megan's face. "I didn't know you were so talented."

Megan and Lili were delighted when Lili's dad offered to make box frames for the collection, a separate frame for each doll. Lili had just learned how to use a wood burning set she received last Christmas. She said she'd write the names of each country at the bottom edge.

When they finished, they took the collection to school where it was placed in the glass showcase near the office — for all to see. Their sudden fame gave them something besides war to think about for a few delicious days.

War Touches Home

THE WORLD, 1942 — Across Europe, freedom fighters
continue their guerrilla activities — Chetniks of
Yugoslavia, Andartes of Greece, the Maquis of France,
"little war makers" of Poland and Russia.

U.S. bombing raids began over Cologne on March 3,
1942, the first of innumerable air raids that destroyed
and devastated major German cities and the armament
works they contained.

COMMODITIES CURTAILED BY WAR WERE ONE THING. But when people close to Lili were affected by it, the war took on another meaning. Two of Lili's cousins went off to war. Don was a flier ferrying bombers from Georgia to Africa. Terry was a sailor stationed aboard the USS Coral Sea, a carrier in the Atlantic. Megan's dad was doing his best for the war effort. He traveled to Army bases on missions that he couldn't talk about. And Harold's older brother lied about his age and joined the Navy.

While Lili envied their adventures, she also knew they were in danger.

"I got another letter from my dad today," Doreen told her SGC friends. "We think he might be in Australia, but we're not sure."

"I'll bet he's mad that he didn't get to go to Holland."

"Yah, but he's still glad he's doing something for the war."

"You miss him?" Megan put her arm around her friend.

"Like crazy."

"Look at all these black blobs." Doreen showed her letter to her friends. She received regular letters from her dad, but lately more and more of the words were blacked out. Censors read all military mail and covered the words that might give families (or spies) clues as to their whereabouts.

As Etta began to add words of reassurance, "He'll be all right. He'll be..." her voice choked and she began to cry.

"What's wrong, Etta?" her friends asked.

"Nothing."

"But you're crying," Megan pointed out.

"Nothing. I'm okay."

"Come on, Etta. Something's wrong. You can tell us, your friends..."

Etta threw her arms around Megan and shook as she sobbed the words, "It's my dad..."

"What happened?" Lili asked. She placed her hand on Etta's shoulder as she spoke.

Etta, warmed by her friends' comfort, lifted her head and sputtered, "I'm worried that my dad might have to go to war." Megan and Lili, sure their fathers wouldn't have to go into service, wrapped their arms around her.

Doreen, asked, "Has he been called up yet? Has he had his Greetings letter?"

"No," Etta whimpered. "But I heard them talking — my mother and father — and I'm afraid he might have to go. Oh, Doreen, how do you stand it... with your dad gone...?"

What comfort could her friends offer? The girls simply held each other and cried together.

Megan and Lili often complained about being girls and too young to get into the war — usually after seeing a movie where Betty Hutton or Rosalind Russell paraded around in designer uniforms and contributed to "the war effort". Such movies always ended with a screen full of smartly marching troops, women as well as men, stepping out to stirring military music.

On those days the girls avoided the mirrored ladies' lounge where they could all too easily see their too-young feminine selves stuck at home while their more patriotic older brothers and sisters got all the glory.

Nevertheless, Lili and Megan screwed up their nerve one Saturday to seek out the WAVE recruiter. It happened during one of their shopping trips on Milwaukee Avenue. The recruiter, seated in a small glassed-in office in the Mall offered them a smiling welcome. After listening to their pleas to "take us; make us sailors," Lt. Barton gently suggested the girls finish school. "Then you would qualify as officers."

Satisfied momentarily, Lili and Megan proudly walked away, appearing at least a foot taller and two years older.

The ongoing war was raising a variety of fears in the minds of Lili and her friends — from fear of spies to fear of being bombed. German accents became more and more unpopular. A German in a movie was too easily identified as the "bad guy". Lili began to have more nightmares — about the smiles of Japanese (like those she saw in movies on the faces of enemies.

Although she knew no Asians, had never seen an Asian, she came to hate the Japanese monsters depicted in the movies who were threatening "our boys in the service". She hated the idea these enemies might come over here and attack America.

"Can we be safe anywhere?" she asked her dad. "Are we safe because we're in the middle of the country?"

"I don't think they'll reach us here, honey. We're not a major industrial center. We're farm country."

"But we produce food for the troops." Lili was sure there was a reason that Milwaukee might be bombed. Why else would the city hold regular air raid practices?

"Still, we're a long way for a bomber to fly — either from Berlin or from Tokyo."

"I've heard about planes that can fly right over the North Pole, from Germany to Wisconsin," she answered. "I read it in the paper."

"But it's not likely." No matter how much her father tried to reassure Lili, she was still unconvinced there was no danger.

Lili's fear spread as schools stepped up the practice air raid alarms, as families kept their windows covered at night, as block wardens patrolled the neighborhoods making sure no light escaped to guide an enemy.

Words that were soon in every child's vocabulary included: *enemy, air raid, bombs, shortages, propaganda, rationing, war effort, strafe,* and *The Duration*. The Duration was as long as it would take to rectify a situation, in this case to end the war.

Lili's yearning pre-teen, romantic heart sang songs of hope, such as "I Walk Alone" (*because to tell you the truth I am lonely*), "When the Lights Go On Again" (*all over the world*), and "There'll Be Bluebirds Over the White Cliffs of Dover" (*tomorrow when the world is free*).

That romantic heart cried itself to sleep some nights. Other nights she lay awake gazing out her window at the dark sky, straining to hear the drone of that plane that might arrive via the North Pole.

Always tomorrow, always the longing, always the waiting for the good times. Someday there will be a world without war, when young men can grow up at home and look forward to a long peaceful life, when children spend each night with their daddies instead of waiting for letters from them, when children won't want for anything — birthday cakes, ice cream, trips to the country, bicycles, real wool clothing. Someday when the ogres of the world are put to rest. Someday "when the world is free".

"I hate the war," Lili wailed to her family and onto the pages of her diary. "I hate the war and wish it was over."

Goodbye Gen. Sherman; Hello Baron vonSteuben

THE WORLD, January, 1943 – The German army has been routed and is surrendering on many points of the Russian front. After fierce night fighting with bayonets, the German army gave up its siege on Stalingrad.

The U.S. offensive in the South Pacific continues following a year of heavy fighting that regained control of Sumatra, Bougainville, New Guinea, and other of the Solomon Islands.

In Asia, the Americans are overcoming the loss of the Burma Road to the Japanese by flying supplies on an around-the-clock schedule "over the hump" from India into China.

THE SIXTH GRADE CLASSES of William T. Sherman School moved away after June 1942. The band of elementary school pupils was promoted to seventh grade and sent on to junior high school, some to Peckham JH and some, like Lili and Megan, to Steuben JH. For the past year they had enjoyed status as the big kids at Sherman, the top of the rank, kings and queens of the hill.

In fact, they had become too big for elementary school. They had to move on. And on they moved from a school named for a Civil War general to Steuben Junior High, named for Major General Baron Friedrich Wilhelm Ludolph Gerhard Augustin von Steuben, a German-born hero of America's Revolutionary War. Would there never be relief from war?

Lili's family moved on too. Their landlady, Gertrude Rosenberg, announced in August that she needed the Deveroux's apartment for a family member. No other explanation. Luckily, George Deveroux found another home for his family just a block away in front of St. Joseph Hospital.

That summer the Deveroux clan moved into their new apartment, this time upstairs, which required the family to walk softly. The people downstairs and the neighbors had young children, which brought Lili prospects of earning babysitting money. (*Babysitting* still wasn't a word. It was called "taking care of children".) The summer they moved in, the neighbor lady brought home a second child and Lili had the chance to care for the newborn baby.

"You seem to have grown up overnight," her mother told her, noticing that Lili had been accepting more responsibility. She willingly did household chores, kept her side of her shared bedroom clean, and even asked her mother to teach her to cook.

"Taking care of children seems to agree with you," her mom told her one afternoon in August.

"I love it. They're such nice people."

"Jewish, aren't they? Strange that we were in a German neighborhood just a block away. Now all our neighbors seem to be Jewish."

"Russian Jewish," Lili corrected. "The Cohens' parents came from Russia. She told me yesterday. Mrs. Cohen's husband is in business with her brothers and her father. Her father doesn't speak any English, and he seems like such a happy man."

"What will she do when you have to go back to school next week?"

"I can still go over after school and on weekends. I'll have plenty of time."

"What kind of children do they have?"

"The little boy calls himself Jimmy Richie Cohen and he's five. The new baby is Renee Diane; they call her 'Cookie'. They're darling children and I love taking care of them."

When school began, the first lesson Lili learned was that junior high brings homework, something she hadn't had to bother with before. But there was another lesson.

Lili and her friends were shocked to discover they were at the bottom of the ranking system again, starting over as the plebes, the newcomers. Baron von Steuben seemingly earned a reputation as a strong military leader by bringing discipline to George Washington's troops. Now again, Steuben Junior High students were learning discipline the hard way.

Lili wondered if there was a correlation between military leaders and education. Was there rhyme or reason why she and her friends were sent to schools named for militarists?

At Steuben, Lili had to learn new ways. She had to deal with lockers and combination locks and homerooms and finding classes and dealing with a half dozen teachers per term. The school had a cafeteria, or at least a lunchroom. But the playground was a small, confined, black-topped space. Where were the jungle gyms?

Walking home from the more distant school became a group event. A large group of students left Steuben each afternoon to walk slowly towards home, cradling their books in both arms and talking over the day's events.

As the group moved away from the school, it became smaller at each street corner as friends waved goodbye and ran towards their homes. Since Megan's corner came up first, the girls of the SGC usually stood there and talked some more.

About the third week of school, a warm September afternoon, Megan and Lili stood at the corner discussing Rudolph Stamm, their math teacher who spoke with a thick German accent. "No, he's too nice to be a German spy," Lili insisted.

"But some of the kids think he is. I think it's awful. I like him." Megan stamped her foot angrily as she spoke.

"Megan..." Lili's voice sounded squeaky as she grabbed her friend's arm.

"Lili, what's wrong?"

"Megan, I'm... I'm not sure. I just feel funny, really weird."

"You look weird too, very pale. Come on over to my house."

The girls walked slowly the few houses down the street, then up the stairs to Megan's room. Lili plopped on the bed and curled her legs up to her chin. "I really hurt, I mean, my stomach..."

"Oh no," Megan gasped as Lili turned on her side, exposing a dark stain on her skirt. "I think you're, you know... you're menstruating."

"What? Oh it can't be."

"Come on. I'll get my mom."

Mom Murphy knew just what to do. She gave the girl a sanitary pad and showed her how to use it, then took the skirt to the kitchen to clean. In very little time, Lili was looking as good as new, although a shade paler, and standing taller.

"This means I'm a woman now," she smiled at Megan. "Do I look different?" Then she thought to ask, "Have you started yet, Megan?"

"No. Mama says it's because I'm anemic. But I should… any day now," she said wistfully. She quickly changed her voice and showered Lili with praise, "You look great, very hubba-hubba, very grownup."

"Aw gee, pal, do you really think so?" Lili mimicked Goofy, the cartoon character. "Aw gee, gosh!"

"How do you feel?"

"My tummy still feels funny, but I'm okay."

"Really, Lil, you do look older. I wish… I wish I'd get grownup too."

"You will."

When Lili arrived home, she didn't mention her new status to her mother. She quietly dug out the box of napkins and the booklet her mother had given her some weeks before. She was old enough to take care of herself now.

THE WAR DRONED ON. Lili's sister Angel, still at Sherman School, reported that her teacher Mr. Kolmas had joined the Navy. The men teachers at Steuben were wondering how soon they would be called. Mr. Rudolph Stamm, who was born in Berlin, wondered if he would be imprisoned. After all, the Japanese-Americans had been incarcerated after Pearl Harbor. The rumors about the witch-hunts for German spies in Milwaukee continued throughout the war, along with debates about whether or not to put German-Americans in prisons, like the Japanese-Americans.

Lili's social science teacher gave assignments that involved reading the daily newspaper, one of the assignments she loved. The *Milwaukee Journal* was full of stories that followed the action both in Europe and in the Pacific. Lili learned the location of islands she never would have heard about if U.S. troops weren't fighting to overtake or hold them — Midway, Guam, Iwo Jima, the Marshalls, the Mariannas, the Philippines, Corregidor, Bataan, New Guinea.

Rumors began to hint about an imminent invasion of Europe, which Hitler held in a stranglehold in 1942 and 1943. Much of the fighting was concentrated in the Mediterranean Sea — North Africa. The Mediterranean countries were teeming with conspirators, freedom fighters, and exiles. Great Britain was suffering. What a way to learn world geography; and the teachers took advantage of it.

Lili wanted to get on with normal living. She held up the newspaper each evening, wondering what it would look like without headlines naming the latest battle, the endless war maps, lists of casualties, and news items about shortages and more rationing. Will "the boys" ever come home? Would young men ever wear anything but uniforms?

"I wonder what the boys our age are feeling?" Lili asked Megan one afternoon as they sauntered home after school, arms loaded with books.

"Scared, I'll bet," Megan replied. "I talked to Harold the other day…"

"You speak to Harold?" Lili's eyes glossed over. She still harbored secret hopes for him.

"Sure, don't you?"

"No, he isn't in any of my classes."

"Anyway, he said he had heard from his older brother. He's in the Navy, you know. And Harold would love to join him."

"I'd be scared witless if I had to go, or even think about going. What must it be like to leave home, to go away without knowing where you're going? What would it feel like to have to wear a uniform all the time? And get up early?"

"I'd worry more about somebody shooting at me," Megan offered. "What would it be like to learn to shoot a gun? To actually shoot another person?"

The girls walked nearly a block in silence, each with her own visions of what it might feel like to go to war, and remembering what the WAVE recruiter had told them.

"What if somebody shot us? And we died? Alone… in pain…" Megan's eyes dramatically misted over and she let the tears trickle down her face. "Oh, Lili, war is awful. I'm glad we're girls and don't have to go off and fight."

"I'm not… glad I'm a girl. I wish I were a boy." Lili was surprised at the way she spit out the words. "I want to get out there and do something. I only wish I were old enough to put on a uniform and fight for my country."

"Even after what Lt. Barton told us?"

"Well yeah! It doesn't look like this war is going to end… ever. You just may have the opportunity. More and more women are joining the WACS and the WAVES. And we'll be out of school in… um… three more years."

"We'd look great in those Navy blue uniforms!"

"You mean like Betty Hutton wore in that movie?"

"Yeah." The girls straightened their shoulders and lifted their chins.

"Lt. Deveroux, let's stop for an ice cream cone. I heard they have a plum royale special this week, and it's not bad with sugar substitutes."

"Gotcha, Lt. Murphy!"

The girls turned toward the drug store and stopped for a treat, their concerns of war momentarily pushed aside.

Boys talked much the same way, some bravely wanting to go, wanting to get into the fray, especially boys with older brothers, cousins, or fathers in the war. There was both romance and pride imbued in the wearing of a uniform. When relatives came home on leave, teenagers crowded about them, envious of the status the serviceman was given. *Serviceman* was an operative word; the only servicewomen Lili or Megan saw were in movies.

Lili's cousin Don, in the Air Force, stopped by the Deveroux home for a brief visit once when he flew into Billy Mitchell Field. Lili thought he looked so handsome in his Air Force uniform — dress pinks and jacket with his new captain's bars and a captain's hat. Although he had told them he was ferrying bombers to South Africa, Lili never felt comfortable knowing about his missions. It wasn't classified information, but still she never mentioned his flights because she didn't want to endanger his life. Loose lips, remember?

Her cousin, Terry, also came to visit on his way from Great Lakes Naval Training Station near Chicago on his way to his new assignment. "Look up your Aunt Rosemary and Uncle George when you get to Milwaukee," his mother had told him. But it was Lili and Angel who were more impressed with their cousin in his chalk-white seaman's uniform.

"I'll send you a pea jacket," he promised Lili. It came in the mail just before Christmas. Never mind the piles of snow along the streets, the cold wind, or her mother's warnings, Lili wore her Navy pea jacket to school. And the head cold that followed was worth every envious look she had received from her classmates.

Later in the war, two more cousins joined the service, one in the Air Force and the other in the Navy. Both were only a few years older than Lili and couldn't get in until almost the end of the war. You can be sure Lili made the most of them when they came to visit wearing their uniforms. A visiting relative in uniform at a junior high school dance meant instant popularity.

Shortages, Trickery, and Victory Gardens

NORTH AFRICA, May 1943 — British troops have broken through to Tunis, dividing Axis forces and taking the port of Bizerte. Field Marshall Rommel surrenders on May 11. By June Africa is back in Allied control; the Suez Canal is safe and the Near East is secure.

JUNIOR HIGH BECAME MORE COMFORTABLE as the months went by. Lili could easily find her way through the many hallways and knew the names of most of her teachers. She came to love the way students changed rooms for every class, giving them opportunities to meet briefly with friends who weren't in other classes. Hallways became the social arena for the seventh graders.

Girls seemed to have one advantage at Steuben — they were the athletes. Lili found she was a good basketball player and a valued member of her team. At first she had wanted to join the gymnastic team, but it was full. Then, her basketball team picked up a first place award on Athletic Honors Day in January 1943. They had won all but two of their games during the season. Girls won a total of 220 honors that day, while the boys won 132. The school didn't have a large football program.

Lili's Girl Scout activities increased. The troop had grown larger. Lili and Megan were among the girls who spent a weekend at Hawthorne House at the edge of

Lake Michigan in February, earning their winter sports badges. Hawthorne was a big old house with a huge fireplace where the girls cooked meals and which provided the heat for sleeping. Bundled in warm blankets, the girls slept near the fire to keep warm.

The cold wind off Lake Michigan lent enthusiasm to the girls who gathered outside the mansion on Saturday morning to learn a new game. Their leader, Mrs. Gruenberg, blew on her mittened hands and slapped them together as she explained the rules.

"The Rabbits — that's this team over here," she pointed to four young girls swaddled in snowsuits and mufflers who were jumping up and down to keep warm. "They'll take off through the woods over there and leave a trail for you to follow." She pointed to another group huddled together, only their pink faces and steam breath showing from behind their woolen clothing. "The trail will lead to a treasure, then back home by a different route," Mrs. Gruenberg continued.

The game originally was to be played in snow, but the harsh winds of Lake Michigan had blown away most of it, and the forest was thick enough to keep most of the snow off the ground. There would be no following tracks in snow that day.

"In fifteen minutes, the Foxes — that's you," she indicated the second group, "will take off after them, looking for clues. Remember, you have to stay together as a team. No going off on your own. We'll keep time after the Rabbits return to see how long it takes the Foxes to find the treasure and return home."

Mrs. G. led the Rabbits off into the woods as Mrs. Johansen, Doreen's mother, led her Foxes around the yard to keep warm. She checked her wristwatch until it was time to leave.

Lili and Megan had decided to split up, Megan as a Rabbit and Lili as a Fox. About ten minutes after the Foxes finally headed towards the woods, Lili remembered the pink confetti. She put her hand in her pocket and moaned, "Oh no!" Only Doreen heard her and asked, "What?"

"Nothing." Lili looked guilty. "This might be harder than I thought," she added.

"How come?" By this time Doreen and Lili had dropped back behind the other Foxes.

"Promise you won't tell your mother?"

"No, course not."

"Look." Lili pulled her hand out of her pocket and showed Doreen a mitten full of pink confetti. She and Megan had sat up in the dark the night before and torn pieces of pink paper into tiny little pieces. The plan was that Lili would be a Rabbit and scatter the pieces along the way. Then Megan, a Fox, would pick up the trail more easily — and faster — and help her team find the treasure and return.

But the sleepy girls had forgotten which team they had decided to be on and had chosen the wrong ones. Megan had become a Rabbit, long disappeared into the woods, without confetti, and Lili had wound up a Fox with no special trail to follow. They'd have to find the regulation trail — a combination of marked trees and written clues.

As they dashed to catch up to the other Foxes, Doreen called to Lili. "Look, Lili, look over here."

The girls spotted an almost unbroken trail of pine cones on the ground. The resourceful Megan had gathered a pocketful of cones at the onset of the game and was picking up more as she moved through the woods. Her trail of pine cones made it easy for the Foxes, now led by Doreen and Lili, to find the treasure. In fact, they almost caught up with the Rabbits as they ran from the woods toward the house.

Inside, a warm fire awaited the girls, with hot cocoa and marshmallows for treats. It wasn't until supper that night that the scheming Lili, Megan, and Doreen confessed their muddled trickery.

"Which proves once again that crime doesn't pay," laughed Mrs. Gruenberg.

"But didn't we all have fun?" The leader waved her arms happily to all her Girl Scouts. No one agreed more than the threesome as they dug into their crusty chicken, cooked over the open fireplace grill. Only someone who has eaten food cooked over an open fire on a very cold night can appreciate just how good it tasted.

SOMETHING ABOUT THE CLOSENESS OF LILI with her friends had turned them into fun-loving schemers. *Crime* wasn't exactly the word they would use to describe their conspiracies. *Intrigue* seemed more appropriate. They usually picked on people outside their group, but once they couldn't resist teasing one of their own. It was during a near epidemic of measles that struck Milwaukee in March 1943.

Lili, her sister Angel, and Megan had already gone through the disease during Lili's first spring in Milwaukee.

Measles and other communicable diseases brought out the Health Department in those days. A quarantine sign on the door meant that nobody could go in or out. No one explained how dads still went to work and mothers still shopped. Angel picked up the virus within a few days and the girls had to stay put for weeks. And just at that time of year when the breezes turned warmer and leaves looked like they might pop out any minute.

At Steuben that spring of 1943, classes were small because of the almost predictable annual siege of measles. It seemed that only the hardy (and the immune) stuck it out. Illusive Lili and Mischievous Megan led the SGC girls to play a trick on the suggestible Minette who often worried needlessly about her health. It started with a casual observation.

"Min, you look a little pale today," Lili noticed during a restroom visit at school.

"Do I?"

"Yeah, is Grandma visiting? Is this your time of the month?" Megan asked.

"No." Minette peered into the mirror and brushed back her dark hair. In contrast, her face did look pale.

"You sure look like something's wrong. Wait a minute, is that a spot?"

Megan was teasing now, but Etta arrived in time to join in, "Whoa, Min, you aren't getting measles, are you?"

The other girls glanced wickedly at each other. One by one they assured Minette she looked poorly. Back in the hall they ran across Beth and brought her into the game. "Don't you think she looks pale, Beth?" Etta asked.

"Yeah, pale," Megan added.

"You do look a bit strange," Beth admitted, adding, "Is that a spot on your cheek? Everyone else has measles. Maybe it's your turn."

The seed had been planted. By noon Minette indeed was feeling ill and went home. To their surprise (and ultimate guilty shame), Min really did have measles. They didn't see her again until the quarantine sign came down.

Minette had been back in school only a few days when the announcement was made of Courtesy Week at Steuben Junior High. The SGC, harboring huge guilt feelings, couldn't help but believe this was especially aimed at them.

The deal was to pass out shields to students caught in the act of being courteous. Seeing the chance for redemption, Lili passed out three the first day, nine the second and seven the third day. Megan gave out a total of twenty-one, and Etta (Minette's best friend) delivered nearly forty over the week. The names of the courteous were collected and placed on a Courtesy Honor Roll, which was plastered in the form of posters all around the school. Twenty-six names in all appeared on the Honor Roll, with the SGC in prominent display. The end result was a heightened appreciation for courtesy at Steuben JH and a resolution from the SGC never never never to play such a mean trick again.

Lili and her classmates often were led on field trips, to such places as Washington Park Zoo, the Whitnal Gardens, the Museum, the downtown library, and City Hall. The main feature at City Hall those days of 1943 was the impressive huge flag of service stars that hung below the rotunda. Of course, as kids do, they also were intrigued with what was called "suicide leap", the hallways that encircled the rotunda.

AS PART OF THE HOMEFRONT WAR EFFORT, Milwaukee was planting victory gardens under the direction of Lili's father's agriculture office. In the rich loamy area of northwestern Milwaukee, several acres had been made available to area residents to plant gardens. Since this was one of her dad's projects, Lili's family chose a fifth of an acre as a kind of demonstration garden. They planted more than the regular carrots and potatos; they grew Chinese celery, red cabbage, seed corn, new varieties of peas and beans, and several exotic plants that Lili had never heard of before.

Lili and Angel drew weekend and summer weeding duty. Their dad would deliver them to the lot in the morning where they hoed and weeded all day. He'd pick them up in the afternoon. The first day the girls went out to weed was a sunny Saturday late in May.

"Bye, Daddy," Lili and Angel called out together as they watched the car drive down the narrow road back toward the highway.

"Come on, Angel, let's get to work," Lili commanded. "Let's make Daddy proud of us."

The younger girl stood watching her father's car disappear. "But we're all alone, Lili," she wailed.

"Oh Angel, don't be a baby. You're too old."

"I'm not a baby,"

"Are too. Okay, if you're not, let's see you work."

Angel, goaded into action, picked up her hoe and set off to weed the pole beans. Both girls knew enough about plants to identify most of them. Besides, the seedlings were just getting their roots under them and the weeds hadn't grown much yet. They worked side by side, moving slowly down each row, until they became thirsty.

"Race you to the water jug," Lili challenged, to let her sister know it was time for a break. The two girls ran to the place next to one of the irrigation ditches that rimmed the field. Since there were no trees for shade, they sat down in the greenery that lined the ditches to enjoy a long drink of water.

"Back to work. We won't stop again until lunch," Lili ordered. The girls returned to their hoeing and worked silently for a time. Angel began to sing one of the songs the family enjoyed when their mother sat down at the piano. "Down by the old mill… stream…" Angel sang. Lili joined in harmonizing loudly. After all, out there in the field under a bright blue sky, in the middle of nowhere with no one around, they could sing as loudly as they wanted.

Singing and hoeing, the girls discovered they actually enjoyed the work. When their grumbling stomachs told them it was time to eat, they were reluctant to stop. But they did.

"I have to go to the bathroom," Angel moaned.

"Go on," Lili responded.

"But there's no bathroom," Angel wailed.

"Over there," her sister pointed to the weeds at the edge of the garden. "Just squat down in the weeds near the ditch. Nobody'll see you. There's nobody here. Remember?"

"You first," Angel said. "I'm scared."

"You're always scared." But Lili realized she had to go too. She chose a spot and worked to loosen her slacks.

When she was through, she waved at Angel and called, "Your turn."

Angel moved deeper into the weeds and repeated her sister's action. She returned to her lunch and they attacked their sandwiches as if they were starving. The sun was higher now and both girls were feeling warmer. They removed their jackets and prepared to return to work.

"Sun's high," Lili called out, much as she had seen farmers do in movies. "Back to the fields." She pulled out her dad's pocket watch and was surprised to see it was only ten o'clock. The sun wasn't as high as it was going to get.

Somehow the girls made it to mid-afternoon, when their father took pity on his daughters and returned early to work with them for a while before taking them home.

Angel chattered endlessly about how hard she had worked and how hot the sun was and how much she had to drink and then, again, how she had to go to the bathroom.

"Over there's a good spot," her father suggested.

But Angel was stubborn. "I have my own place," she said and strutted off. It wasn't until she returned that her dad noticed where she had been.

"Oh my, have to get you right home," he said, noticing how Angel was rubbing at her backside.

"What's wrong, Daddy," Lili asked, noticing her father's concern.

"Nettles."

"Nettles? What are they?"

"Those weeds… over there… where Angel was squatting. Those are nettles. Very nasty little weeds. They'll make you itch like crazy."

Angel began to cry, still rubbing her bottom. "I itch, bad, already."

"Oh, not that soon. It takes a few hours. But you'll feel them soon. Let's get you home."

And off they went, Angel wailing, Lili laughing (until she remembered she had sat in the same place), and their dad driving as fast as he could to reach home and calamine lotion. It took only that lone encounter with the itchy things to keep the girls away from nettles forever.

The incident left the Deveroux sisters with opposite reactions. Lili received her love of gardening from those peaceful days hoeing in the fields — where the Mayfield Shopping Center now sits. Angel, in later years, identified the experience as the basis for her hatred of gardening.

Even their mom got into the gardening thing. The girls giggled, but thought their mother looked real groovy the day she donned a pair of overalls and took to the fields. Lili had never seen her mother wear anything but housedresses or church dresses. But there she was, all five feet of her, wallowing about in too-large overalls in their Victory Garden.

With the success of his own garden, and as Milwaukee County Agent, Lili's dad was a guest speaker at a Steuben assembly the following spring, encouraging pupils to start Victory Gardens and keep them up during the summer.

Lili sat slumped in her seat as her father took the stage and was introduced. Having your dad speak to an auditorium full of schoolmates is probably the most embarrassing moment in a teenager's life. Still, she admitted she was proud of his speech and proud of what he was doing for the war effort.

The Victory Garden Festival at Steuben was held in the fall. Students brought and displayed the vegetables they had grown over the summer and received defense stamps as prizes. Lili won two 50-cent grand prizes and a first prize for the onions and potatos she had grown. She received a first prize for cucumbers and second prize for pumpkins, a total of $1.85 in defense stamps. She couldn't have been happier.

That was also the summer that Megan and Lili took part in a Cherry Pageant, a June celebration at Sherman Park that drew crowds of kids and adults alike. Somehow, the girls caught the attention of reporters who took their pictures. Once again the friends appeared together in both the *Milwaukee Sentinel* and the *Milwaukee Journal*.

Rationing continued, with shortages getting shorter in 1943. Chocolate, vanilla, and sugar were becoming impossible to find. Bakeries were selling mostly bread and buns. Some of them were coming up with creative alternatives to cakes and pies. Eggs and milk played a big role in most of Lili's desserts. How lucky she was to live in Wisconsin, The Dairy State.

Fat rendering became valuable to the war effort, providing precious glycerin to make explosives. Lili's mother kept a can behind the stove where all fat was poured after use. Lili was in charge of turning in the filled container, receiving 10 cents for each can.

Not that there was much fat. Pork was cheap those days, more available than beef, and supplied most of the fat collected. Chicken also was in bigger supply than beef. With the meat shortage, sausages and wursts were prized table fare in Milwaukee. Lili's mother tried to cook fish, which seemed in good supply. She asked Mrs. Cohen to teach her how to cook the kind of fish her Jewish neighbors enjoyed, but Rosemary Deveroux never got the hang of it. As hard as her mother tried to cook gefilte fish, it never tasted the way Mrs. Cohen cooked it.

Travel of any great distance was impossible because of gas rationing. Sunday drives were out. Reading was in. Lili wallowed in her love of books. She and Megan haunted the library on Center Street on Saturdays since the schools didn't have libraries. Although much of the reading was for school, they managed to include a few Nancy Drew mysteries and other teenage books in their selections. Lili began to collect the works of Louisa May Alcott and her personal library grew during those years.

Lili also improved her knitting. Encouraged by Miss Nicoud at Sherman School, Lili continued to knit, turning out several plain scarves and watch caps for the Red Cross over the junior high years. Spurred by the fashion for school sweaters, she started a sweater for herself. She already had knit pairs of bobby sox for herself and her friends. The sweater, light blue, took most of the seventh and eighth grades to finish, but she finally wore it to school.

D-Day and Bean Camp

ROME June 4, 1944 — Allied forces entered Rome today, ousting the Germans from most of southern Italy. American troops invaded Sicily in July 1943 and landed troops at Anzio in January 1944.

Two days later, on June 6 — D-Day — Allied troops landed on the shores of France and began the liberation of Europe.

THE WINTER SNOWS HAD MELTED EARLY in 1944 and Steuben Junior High Schoolers celebrated with a Spring Fair. The war news was sprinkled with hope. Rumors of an imminent invasion of Europe were spreading across the Allied countries and even smuggled into the imprisoned nations of Europe.

German cities were feeling the devastation of heavy bombing. Even Berlin was being turned into piles of rubble. If ever there was a depth to the disregard for human life and civility in the world, Lili was sure it happened during the Christmas and Hanukkah season of 1943.

The longed-for news began to trickle in — June 6, 1944, the week after Lili and Megan finished seventh grade.

"Have you heard?" Megan screamed at Lili as the two met on a day early in June to work on their dolls. They were working on American costumes by this time.

"Heard what?"

"Heard about the invasion." Breathless with good news, she repeated what she and her mother had heard on the radio. "Waves and waves of our soldiers are landing on the beaches of France. Ike sent over planes and ships and troops to free Europe!" Megan loved to refer to General Eisenhower by his nickname, since he looked so much like her father.

The girls hugged each other, sure now that the long war was going to end.

But not just yet.

The long awaited invasion under General Eisenhower began on the shores of France on June 6 and soldiers started their march across the continent, scattering the Nazis in front of them. While the Pacific battlefields were still bloody, there seemed to be a sense that the tide had turned there as well.

Meanwhile, support for the war effort never flagged. A hopeful homefront tightened their belts and never missed a beat of rivets on war equipment or stitches of hand-knit sweaters and caps.

Bolstered by her success at the family Victory Garden, Lili turned over the weeds to her sister Angel that summer of 1944 and trundled off to Bean Camp. With many farm workers off to war, civilians were recruited to harvest food. Camps were set up to accommodate the women and young people who volunteered.

Lili's dad supervised a few of the civilian crop harvesting camps as part of his work with the University of Wisconsin Extension Department. It was he who suggested that Lili sign up for the camp. "It'll be good experience in meeting other people. Besides, you'll be supporting the war effort."

The camp was in Hayward, a small town in the middle of fir trees and fishing ponds in northern Wisconsin. The area boasted huge vegetable farms.

Lili arrived with her father and was led to a very plain wooden bunkhouse. She met other girls, mostly older than she was, and managed to latch onto a top bunk for herself. She unpacked, trying bravely to ignore the fact her father was going to leave at the end of the day and she would be alone with strangers.

However, she tried to think like Megan and boldly set out to make friends. By suppertime, she barely noticed him leave, tossing him a kiss and rejoining her newfound friends for an evening of campfire singing and story telling.

The next day the work began very early and it was hard, exhausting the girls at the end of their long days. They were transported at sunrise to the fields in trucks, spent the day scooting along the long rows of string beans, picking and tossing beans into bags, dumping the bags into huge vats, and returning to the endless rows to pick more beans.

The first few nights, the girls fell into their bunks after supper. As they hardened to the work, they found new energy at night to walk into town and check it out. They found few people their age, but they did manage to discover an ice cream store that fit their moods.

One noon as the girls pulled themselves toward the work truck to claim their box lunches, one of them shouted, "Hey look, Indians." She pointed to a group of American Indian women sitting along a fence at the side of the field.

"Are they picking beans too?"

"Looks like they're eating lunch."

"They must be working in that field over there."

The girls cradled their lunches under one arm and took a few cautious steps toward the Indians. "They don't belong here," said the girl they called Babe. "They belong back on the reservation."

"Don't," said Lili, feeling protective. "Leave them alone. They're just eating."

"But look what they're eating," Babe said. "What is it?"

Lili strained her eyes. What they were eating certainly were not sandwiches. Nor fruit. Their food appeared gray. The women themselves sat cross-legged, heads bowed, appearing not to notice the girls.

"My god, they're eating potatos. Cold potatos," shrieked Babe.

"How can they work with that kind of food?" asked the girl called Carly. "Ugh! That's awful."

"Let's just eat our lunch and leave them alone," Lili repeated.

That's what she said. What she wanted to do was run over to these women and share her lunch, hug them, assure them the girls were stupid, and beg the crew leader to feed the women a decent meal. But she held her tongue.

That evening she sat alone in the bunkhouse and wrote a long letter to Megan. Babe and Carly and the others had gone off to town for ice cream. Lili had lost her appetite.

Dear Megan, she began the letter. She played with the pencil as she tried to compose the words she wanted to put down.

I had the most amazing experience today. Now I know I'm really an Indian. I know what it feels like to be Indian. She paused, wondering if Megan would understand what she was trying to say.

We saw a group of Indian ladies at the bean field. I wondered if they were Chippewas. The other girls started to make fun of them. And I felt awful. You wouldn't believe how poor they were. They wore raggy clothes and tied up their hair with rags and they ate cold potatos.

Lili was surprised at the tears that filled her eyes. *I felt so sad for them. And then I began to feel sad for me. Because I am Indian too.*

She sat back on her bunk and let the tears finish the ride down her cheeks, around her mouth, and onto her chin. Her shoulders shook with the sobs, and she covered her head with her arms and wept for all the Indians who were poor, all the people in the world who were poor and hurting, all the soldiers fighting a dreadful war, all the lonely sisters and daughters and mothers who would never see their boys again. And she wept for herself, alone among strangers, and knowing she was part Indian.

The next day, the Indian women didn't appear and Lili was just as glad they didn't. She had decided to tell her co-workers that she was Indian herself — if the subject had come up again.

At the end of two weeks, Lili had enough of the hard work and the lonliness. When her dad came for an inspection, she gave up and begged him to take her home with him. While she was growing up very fast, she was still too young to be out on her own. She felt regret briefly as she told her new friends goodbye, but she sang all during the ride home.

WITH THE INVASION OF FRANCE and the turning of the tide of war in late 1944, Lili, her family and friends, and the entire nation, seemed to have locked step in the final march against dictators. Shortages, discomfort, losses had become an accepted part of living. Belts had been tightened almost to the limit, but people always seemed to manage one more notch.

More and more gold stars appeared on small window flags, icons to the men and women who had given their lives for their country. The heels of Americans seemed to dig deeper into the determination to liberate the word from tyranny.

Lili kept busy with Girl Scouts. Her troop became an Air Cadets Troop and studied the dynamics of airplanes and flying. They took a memorable trip to Billy Mitchell Airfield where the girls had a chance to experience the sensation of flying in a Link Trainer. Lili was thrilled with her "flight". As she crawled out of the cockpit, she vowed to learn to fly as soon as possible

Lili discovered she was good at tumbling, an art that came to be known as gymnastics, and finally joined the team. Harold and other Steuben boys developed a winning basketball team, giving Lili and her tumbling team further motivation to develop a demonstration routine to perform during halftimes. Incidentally, Harold was facing competition in Lili's heart from a boy named David, who also, happily, played basketball.

During the games, Lili watched from the sidelines as both her young men raced back and forth across the gym.

At halftime, Lili and her team kept the crowd's attention with feats of daring on rings and mats and gymnastic horses. Exercise and wild teenage enthusiasm blocked out the war for a few hours.

Goodbye President Roosevelt; Goodbye War

PRAGUE, CZECHOSLOVAKIA May 8, 1945 —
German troops finally laid down their arms today as
fighting ends in Europe. Millions of German soldiers
attempted to flee to the west to escape being taken
captive by Russian troops. The west is calling this V-E
Day.

IT WAS FOLLOWING THE BASKETBALL SEASON, in the spring
of 1945 that America's leader, President Franklin D.
Roosevelt, died unexpectedly in Warm Springs, Georgia,
the end of an era.

When they heard of his death at school that
Thursday (April 12), Lili and Megan hugged each other
and cried as if they had lost their own fathers. Neither
had known any other President and felt deeply the death
of this world leader who had steered them through a
war.

Just as quickly, came the end of the war in Europe
when Germany surrendered on May 7. On V-E Day,
Tuesday, May 8, Steuben Junior High joined the rest of
the country to celebrate with an assembly service of
thanksgiving. Lili played with the school orchestra in a
pop concert. At noon a whistle ended all school and
work for the day.

That evening the Deveroux family attended church, along with families across the country and around the world. The war in Europe had ended.

THE MILWAUKEE DAYS WERE OVER for Lili and her family. George Deveroux announced he had taken a job in Eau Claire, in northern Wisconsin; the family would be moving away at the end of the 1945 school year. Lili felt devastated. In September her class would move on to Washington High School without her.

The SGC hastily called a meeting as soon as Lili related the news. Not only did the Sassy Seven appear for a going away party hastily announced by Megan, but so did some of Lili's friends on the tumbling team, in Girl Scouts, from church, and some new friends from Steuben.

"We aren't going to make speeches or cry," Megan told Lili as she arrived at Megan's home for the party. But cry they did. As each guest arrived, Lili seemed more and more surprised to find how many friends she had collected in just five years.

Mrs. Murphy prepared her best spaghetti (made with zucchini instead of meat) and then presented Lili with a big cake sweetened with fruit and raisins. At sight of the cake, Lili managed, "Aw, you shouldn't have..." to Mrs. Murphy while big tears rolled down both their cheeks.

The rest of the evening the girls kept up a continuous round of "Do you remember when..." and "I'll never forget the time..."

When the evening came to a close, Megan held her friend's hand and presented her with a gift "from all of us."

"Oooh, this is too much," Lili said as she hugged Megan. "I'll never forget any of you."

"You can't. Not when you see your present," Minette called to Lili.

Lili tore open the wrapping and pulled the cover from the box. Inside lay a bracelet made of six small silver links. On each was inscribed the name of one of the SGC. "It's beautiful," Lili sobbed. "Oh, I'll remember all of you, but I won't need a bracelet to do it. You're such good friends…" but she couldn't continue. FIfteen-year-old girls form bonds out of tears that nobody can break.

Megan and Lili spent one last sleep-over and cried all night. Then the Deveroux family moved away.

Megan visited Lili in July that summer, joining the family for a week of swimming and fishing at Tainter Lake. (The next year, Lili traveled by bus to visit Megan in Milwaukee. Her parents let her make the trip on a school day so she could spend time with her friends at Washington High.)

On August 6, 1945, Lili read in the newspapers about something called an *atom bomb* that had been exploded over the Japanese city of Hiroshima. She barely noticed, not realizing the gravity of the event. When reports indicated how calamitous was the dropping of that bomb, and the one on August 9 on Nagasaki, Lili hoped only for the end of this war in the Pacific.

By V-J day, Lili had moved and was getting to know her way around the new town. The war in the Pacific ended on August 14 with the first reports at 6 p.m. of a

Japanese surrender. Auto horns tooted in the streets; children yelled… heck, everyone yelled! Lili was working at a Girl Scout day-camp that summer. On the way home that evening she joined the celebrations. Overwhelmed with the long-awaited event, Lili roamed the streets dazed. That night the 15-year-old wrote in her diary, simply, "I was late for supper. The war's over."

No longer content to be an outsider, Lili joined a new Girl Scout troop and soon made new friends — Ginny and Sally and Pat and Wanda and Evelyn. The girls took a bike hike the morning of August 15 as the formal surrender took place on the carrier USS Missouri. Then the troop attended church at noon together.

A holiday atmosphere filled the town, the country — and the world. Starting in the afternoon, a dance filled downtown streets and continued on into the night. This time Lili wrote in her diary, "My friends and I had to go see what was going on. We danced with complete strangers and had a glorious time."

A Lifetime Later

THE SCHOOL BELL RINGS, startling Lili Deveroux who stands transfixed on the second floor of William T. Sherman Elementary School, 60 years after she had first entered the building. It is summer; school is out, but the bells continue to ring.

Words begin to pour into Lili's head as she walks slowly down the terrazzo stairs and back to her end-of-the-century world. She knows she'll have to write down the words so they won't get lost.

The war has been over for more than half a century. America fought the fight of its lifetime on behalf of the free world and won — on two fronts that covered the entire world.

Lili recalls something she once heard Maxine Andrews, of the Andrews Sisters, explain on a television show: "Everybody... I think everybody in their hearts was trying to save their country. I think it's one of the first times that Americans went to war with the idea that we could be invaded, that we were vulnerable."

At the edge of a new century, the United States remained uninvaded, yet still vulnerable. Now the reasons are different. Time, travel, and technology have shrunk the world. Words like *overseas* and *half a world away* don't apply anymore. Any place in the world is only hours away from anyplace else.

Many of Lili's Milwaukee friends contributed their memories to this book. Lili entered Milwaukee at the start of the war in Europe and left just as it was ending. Her memories of Milwaukee are only of those war years.

For most of her friends, the situation was different. Those who grew up in Milwaukee remember the times before and after the war. For them, the war was just a part of their Milwaukee lives. For Lili it was the whole experience.

All of this may explain why she feels so strongly about this story, not just because it brings back memories for those who lived them, but because it tells the story to those who never went through a war that affected them directly. World War II belongs as much to those kids who saved and recycled and did without and bought defense stamps and who cheered their relatives in the service, and wept for them, as it does to those who fought at the front. They were the kids of World War II.

Those who survived World War II, wherever they lived then, can identify with today's children of Korea, Vietnam, Ireland, Israel, Palestine, Russia, Yugoslavia, Panama, Nicaragua, China, Iran, Iraq, Afghanistan, Syria, and all the other places of unrest in the world.

The kids at William T. Sherman Elementary School knew how that awful war affected children who were nowhere near the bombs. What must it be like for those who hear the bombs every day?

Not one day goes by that Lili doesn't look at a newspaper — mostly without the war maps now and without the lists of casualties, the headlines depicting battles in strange places — and, thank god, she doesn't have to wonder how the front page would look if this country were in the midst of another struggle like World War II.

She is concerned, however, at the other battles that rage across newspaper headlines: terrorist attacks, children killing and being killed by handguns, women mutilated, violence that still occupies newspaper space. Sometimes she feels almost as if the country is still fighting a war.

As a journalist — yes, Lili became a newspaper reporter and then newspaper editor — she realizes that the words "nothing happened today" do not draw readers. Still, she notes the senselessness of violence, the futility of fighting, and the death of society that accompanies any violence.

General Sherman was right. "War is hell", and still is. Not only for those in the battle, but for those who suffer the losses of family, those who perceive threats to themselves, and those who only read about it.

If we have choices — and we certainly have been given choice as part of our humanity — why would anyone ever consider waging war again?

Life Should Feel Like
You Want to Shout
(Notes from the Author)

SUMMER 1988, IF YOU REMEMBER, was the hottest that Milwaukee could ever recall. I returned to Milwaukee for the first time in many years — a sort of pilgrimage on my way to the 40th reunion of my high school graduating class at Fort Atkinson (WI). The trip didn't turn out as complete as I had planned.

In the heat I snapped a few pictures of my two former homes on 50th Street, Sherman and Steuben schools, and my old church; I drove through Washington Park (where's the zoo?), past the shuttered Uptown Theater, skipped through the phone book (my "Harold" wasn't there) and headed for Fort Atkinson, an air conditioned motel, and my high school graduating class reunion. When my pilgrimage ended, I returned home to Washington State, developed my pictures, and went back to work.

My Fort Atkinson High School graduating class meets every five years; I assumed Washington High School's did too. I would have graduated from Washington in 1948 if I had stayed in Milwaukee, and I surmised that my elementary school classmates would be reuniting the same time my Fort Atkinson classmates were.

In a streak of bright ideas, I decided in 1993 to return to Wisconsin and join celebrations at both of "my high schools", the one I attended in Fort Atkinson and the one I might have attended in Milwaukee. I planned to visit Washington High School to see if I could obtain a list of people graduating the same year I did. If I was lucky, I might find some of my women friends' married names and most certainly, some of the men who were schoolmates at Sherman Elementary.

After visiting attending a family reunion in River Falls, I drove straight to Milwaukee and got to work. Early Monday morning I arrived on the steps of Washington High and was directed to the computer department operated by Joseph W. Kmoch, Systems Manager. I hit pay dirt!

Joe handed me my precious list of 1948 graduates, both January and June. (I had forgotten about the two semester system.) I raced through it expectantly, calling out names as I recognized them. Many still lived in the Milwaukee area. I planned to call them that very day.

What about "Harold"? my mind asked. Would he possibly still live around here, someplace close to Milwaukee? Was he even alive? "Harold" was the dashing boy whose sparkling dark eyes had caught the attention of every girl who ever went to school with him. (Every class seems to have one of those guys.)

I flipped pages spotting many familiar names. This one's in Illinois. This one's in California. Hey, she's right here in Milwaukee; I can call her today.

Then I saw it — "Harold". My eye moved across the columns to the address. What? It couldn't be! Of all the ironies: His address was in Tacoma, Washington, just a few blocks from my own home.

"You won't believe this," I shrieked my good news at Joe, spilling out the amazing coincidence. Suddenly I couldn't wait to get home.

However, I had a few more days to spend in Milwaukee before heading to the Fort Atkinson reunion (my Washington High class wouldn't meet for another five years). I spent those three days well. I called several familiar names on the list and set up appointments to meet a few of them. My close girlfriend, Ruth Bernstein, was married to another classmate, Norbert Sweet. We planned to meet the next evening. That afternoon I drove out to Brookfield to visit with Hedwig Diers. (She didn't attend Sherman School, but was a close friend from Steuben.)

I arranged to have lunch with Roberta Froelich and Corrine Jacobson. I left messages with Sheldon Schnoll and Romaine Fisher, who Ruth had reached before I did. She invited Romaine to join us at the Sweets' home where we spent a delicious evening recalling Sherman School. I chatted briefly with Sheldon over the telephone.

From the airport, I finally reached Harvey Allisch, who I remembered as a close friend of Eleanor Lamb, my best friend. He remembered me and yes, he remembered Sherman Elementary — fondly. We chatted for several minutes trying to cover a 45-year interim.

You can't imagine the joy at re-meeting and spending time with people I hadn't seen for five decades and with whom I once felt very close. It's very easy to slip back into the comfort of friends. We gabbed about other friends, teachers, our memories of grade school. We updated each other on our families, careers, lives. We stared at faces that were at once different yet familiar, faces that looked less distant as the evening went on.

And the voices! Voices don't change much, their cadence, emphasis, tone, rhythm, accent. How easy to close my eyes and feel the fifty years disappear.

Yes, they remembered too — some with prompting. One memory led to another, and then another.

At the time I wasn't sure why I was contacting these dear friends, nor what I would do with the precious memories we were dredging up. While one instinct suggested nobody cared and I should shut up, something within me said it was important.

I decided to follow the voice inside telling me: Life should feel like you want to shout!

And shouting is what I felt like doing about William T. Sherman School, my friends, my teachers, and my experiences.

What you read here is a fictional story derived from essays written over the years, updated, and corrected with the help of friends: Ruth Bernstein Sweet, Norbert Sweet, Romaine Fisher Backer, Roberta Froelich Wegener, Corinne Jacobson Horn, Hedwig Diers Smith, Mary Demeter Thurrell, Doris Pratt Reed (d. 1998), Gordon Kaiser, Harvey Allisch, and Sheldon Schnoll (d. 1995).

My dear friend, Ruthie, no longer is with us, nor is her husband Norbert Sweet.

My very first best-friend, "Megan" was Eleanor Lamb, who died much too soon, at the age of 22.

Two weeks after I returned home, I connected with "Harold" and we met for a pleasant coffee to share memories.

I went to work, and when I returned to my two high schools five years later for our 50th year reunion, I took along the limited edition of this book, wrapped in gold paper, for the friends I had connected with — at both schools.

BUT WHAT HAPPENED TO THOSE DEVOTED TEACHERS? The Milwaukee School District was helpful in finding out about the teachers of William T. Sherman Elementary School. Here's what turned up:

LOUIS ULRICH was principal of Sherman School from January 1924 until his retirement on June 17, 1959. I remembered that he wrote an arithmetic book, *Understanding Arithmetic 7* (1956) and tried out his theories on the students of Mr. Kolmas' fifth grade class.

LILLIAN HORNE, my fourth grade teacher and friend of my grandmother, began teaching at Sherman School in September 1928. She retired in June 1966 and died January 10, 1969.

MARY NICOUD, my fifth grade teacher, came to Sherman School in June 1926, transferred to the 95th Street School in February 1956, and retired in January 1970.

HARRY R. KOLMAS, my other fifth grade teacher, came to Sherman shortly after his marriage in 1938. He served in the Navy during World War II and returned to teach at Sherman until his retirement. He died about 1987. His wife, Elizabeth, spoke to me in 1993, saying how much her husband enjoyed teaching and how proud he was of his students. He kept all their pictures and notes of their achievements, she said.

LEA MILTON, my sixth grade teacher, though never one of my favorites, taught me how to deal with people I didn't agree with. She also taught me how difficult it is to learn when personalities clash. She taught at Sherman School from January 1927 until her death on December 24, 1956.

RUTH SCHLUETER, the teacher I wish I'd had in sixth grade, spent her entire teaching career at Sherman School, from November 1921 until her retirement in May 1967.

PHILIP ZAREM, another sixth grade teacher, directed the school's safety cadets. I also talked with his wife, Sarah, who said he died about 1980. He had become vice principal before his retirement.

ONE MORE NOTE: If you are concerned about the spelling of such words as *heros, echos, potatos, tomatos, Negros,* you may want to pick up a copy of the author's latest grammar book, *American-English: The Official Guide* (2016), or the earlier *Anarchist's Guide to Grammar* (2012) or *Grammar For Grownups* (HarperCollins, 1993, still available) where you'll discover the "Guideline of Plural Nouns Ending in O".

The Author

Val all grown up

Val in 5th grade

VAL DUMOND has grown up to live a full and fascinating life that has taken her to exotic countries and throughout her magnificent native land, the U.S. of A. She now lives near her two beloved grownup children, Frederick and Lisbeth, in the Pacific Northwest where she continues to keep a diary, write books, edit them for others, and help other writers publish their books.

If you lived through World War II, or if you ever attended Sherman School or lived in that northwest Milwaukee neighborhood — as she did — you'll recognize many of the places and people and events of those tumultuous years.

Her pilgrimage continues. After all, life is a pilgrimage. She's always seeking new sights and remembering old ones. She'd love to hear from you and share your memories of William T. Sherman Elementary School… or wherever.

Val Dumond can be reached at her website: www.valdlumond.com, Twitter, LinkedIn, and Facebook.

www.ingramcontent.com/pod-product-compliance
Lightning Source LLC
Chambersburg PA
CBHW052031020726
47501CB00004B/1364